The Prophecy of Apollo

Book III
Master Mage of Rome Series

D.W. FRAUENFELDER

BREAKFAST WITH PANDORA BOOKS

in association with

True North Writers & Publishers Co-operative

Houston, Texas

ISBN: 0-9966933-6-3
ISBN-13: 978-0-9966933-6-3

Cover art and formatting by Streetlight Graphics

streetlightgraphics.com

TO RICHARD
amico optimo

CONTENTS

THE PROPHECY OF APOLLO

::I::

On a night in early April in his nineteenth year, a dream woke Lucius Junius Brutus from a sound sleep.

Lucius was awake and aware immediately, in that very peculiar and occasional way, of seeming to be wide awake while dreaming and then waking in that same state.

A grammarstone lay by his hand, next to the cot where he slept every night in the cave of Numa Pompilius. He left the stones next to his hand in case there was need of them.

And there was need of them.

"*Lucs mani magi magistri*," he whispered as he held the stone in the well of his palm. *May there be light in the hand of the master mage.*

Light sparkled from the stone and filled the room.

Lucius shielded his face with an arm and held up the other until he became used to the light. He then pulled on his cloak, picked up his *baculum*, his staff of power, and, with the help of the light, made his way out of the cave.

It was early morning, but with no hint of dawn yet. The air

was cool and dry, touched with the slightest of breezes, sweet with the smell of ryegrass and wildflowers. In the distance, a nightingale called.

It was the beginning of sailing season, the month of Aprilis, a time of warm breezes, green grass baking to brown in the joy of the strengthening sun. Summer with its scorching heat was still some time away and at night a chill still came as a guest, soon to be on its way.

"A snake," Lucius whispered as he half-ran, half-walked up the hill toward the grammarstone quarry and the entrance to the Spirit World, from where the prodigies of Rome found their way into ours.

It was clear from the dream what Lucius must do. He had seen in the dream a serpent, six feet long and with sharp, venom-dripping fangs, emerging from the central pillar of the palace of Lucius Tarquinius, King of Rome.

The serpent was sent to kill the king.

Lucius must stop the snake.

Lucius made a grammar that allowed him to fly the final distance between the entrance of the quarry and the cleft in the rock he had investigated years ago under the guidance of his teacher, Glyph. He still used it as a way in to the Spirit World, whenever he received an alert about a danger to the city of Rome. He scrambled inside the first cave through the cleft, the light illuminating the rock walls.

Nothing seemed amiss, as far as he could tell. But the feeling of being in a dream while he was awake, or being awake in a dream, was still with him, and in the shadows of the cave, he felt unsure of his senses.

Lucius alit on the gravelly floor of the cave and set out

investigating the chambers that were still in this world. Now and then he might find a prodigy had crossed over from the Spirit World but was still inside the caves. Sometimes he would wait for the prodigy to cross over and battle it then. Less often he would make a portal to the world and attack the prodigy on its own ground.

But there was something different about this one.

The air in the caves was always musty from the drip of water from some crack, and when there was a prodigy present Lucius could smell something like that damp pungent smell of an approaching thunderstorm. Or there might be a whiff of sulfur, or rotting flesh, depending on what had freed itself from Spirit and become Real.

This time there was nothing. The air smelled of the mildew that was always present, but otherwise was clean, no other scents.

Had the prodigy already left the cave? Or perhaps had not gotten there yet? Lucius thought for a minute that he might need to go across worlds and investigate.

No smell?

But it had seemed so close.

Then he realized something that turned his mind away from the prodigy itself.

Kill the king?

Lucius thought hard for a moment, fighting the sleep that had so recently gripped him. When he had dreams of prodigies, he almost always dreamed of what they were: a monster, a rain of blood, a plague. He almost never also dreamed of what the prodigy was sent to do. There was just a threat, a sense of danger.

But this dream was clearly about the king, Tarquinius, the Etruscan. The one Lucius had one day determined to overthrow when the time was right.

If a serpent was sent to kill the king, might that not be a good thing? Might it not make it easier for Lucius to accomplish what he wanted, to make Rome Roman again and give the power of rule to its people?

Lucius shook his head as if to clear it. His empty stomach turned over. He had woken up too quickly.

It was then that the snake struck.

The snake was the color of the rocks and dirt where it lay coiled in a corner, waiting for Lucius to approach. It made no sound and had no scent that Lucius could perceive, and when it struck, it struck so fast that Lucius had no time to bring up his *baculum* and utter a grammar.

The fangs went deep into Lucius' thigh and just as quickly the snake recoiled and leapt forward, past Lucius and toward the hole in the rock.

Lucius cried out in pain and astonishment and hit the ground hard, as if his legs had been swept from underneath by the hand of a giant. He let go of the *baculum*, fell on his face, tasted gravel and dust; the twin puncture of the fangs radiated pain.

Worse, the venom pumped into his body immediately began to numb his legs.

"*Baculum*," he said to himself, scrabbling with both hands at his side in case he could pick up the staff quickly. There was just time to throw a grammarstone at the snake with some words of attack, and then a healing grammar for himself.

There was just time, that is, if the venom did not paralyze

his arms and tongue.

"*Baculum mani!*" Lucius cried. *May the staff be in my hand.*

This was a grammar that was easily accomplished in this place where the magic of the grammarstones was so strong. The *baculum* stood up straight from where it lay, eight feet away, and whirled end over end, the tapered end nesting in Lucius' palm.

Lucius swiveled up onto one knee, bracing himself with an arm. He chambered a grammarstone in the knob of the *baculum* and let it go toward the retreating snake, crying as he did, "*Lapis serpentem!*" *May the stone attack the snake.*

It was a simple grammar, one that would have easily taken care of a real snake. It would have been good enough to stop a spirit snake as well.

But this opponent was stronger.

The grammarstone flew directly up and towards the ceiling. In less than the blink of an eye there was a cracking sound as a chunk of rock disengaged from the cavern ceiling. The rock, the shape of a dinner plate but three times as wide, came hurtling down.

The rock should have easily crushed the snake under its weight. It did, in fact, hit the floor with a deafening roar, and shattered into a thousand pieces.

Lucius had to shield his face from dust and rocks. But when the dust settled and he could see again, the snake could be seen slithering up the side of the cliff, not directly up but sideways, in the grooves of the rock. What's more, the snake glowed, its scales silvery where they had been dull before.

"It can't be," Lucius said, and readied another grammar. This one would make no mistake. He'd summon an axe to chop off the snake's head.

But the venom had done its quick work.

The *baculum* fell from Lucius' hand. He tried to stand up, found he couldn't feel his legs, found one hand completely numb and the other almost so. The arm he'd used to brace himself slackened, and he fell again, this time onto his back. He was a turtle, helpless.

With the last of his strength and the feeling in the fingers of one hand, he clutched a jagged piece of rock and thrust it into his mouth. He didn't need to swallow the raw grammarstone to make the grammar work, but it would help to have it as close as possible to its target.

"*Venenum serpentis...*" he gurgled. *May the venom of the serpent...*

What grammar to use? His mind was failing him. Something about medicine or water or weakening...

As he lost consciousness, he said, "*mago magistro...*" *for the master mage.*

"*Mutatom.*"

Be changed.

That was all he could do.

It was the last thing he did.

::II::

"Lucius! Master!"

It was a voice that seemed to be coming from a long way away, in darkness.

Lucius tried to open his eyes. They blinked. The darkness did not recede. Was it night?

"Master, can you hear me?"

"Sssssnak..." Lucius slurred. His tongue was heavy, dry.

Someone patted his cheeks. "Lucius?"

This voice he recognized. D—D—someone with a name that began with that letter. It was a she. A welcome voice. A voice of comfort and friendship. Love.

"Dem... Dem..."

"Yes, Demetria, Lucius. Logo's here, too. Can you hear us?"

"Give him some water."

Lucius felt his head being propped up, lips being parted. A trickle of water ran along his tongue. He coughed, but swallowed.

"Snake!" Lucius whispered hoarsely.

"It's all right, Lucius. We found you and you're going to be all right." This from the voice of Demetria, though Lucius still could not see her. He was no longer in the cave. The smell of it had been replaced with that of burning oil, the oil used in lamps in the cave of Numa Pompilius.

"Did you battle a prodigy, master?" This was Logophilus, the companion of Glyph, who kept the shrine.

Lucius nodded. "Snake!" he said again, and finding his tongue almost useless, asked for water again.

"Here it is. Lie back. Relax. You're lucky to be alive, I think."

Lucius took a bigger drink, and found he could move his arm. He reached out, put his hand in Demetria's, taking strength from her presence. "Thank you!"

The young Greek put her face to his and kissed him near his ear. The familiar floral smell of olive oil and lavender that she rubbed on her skin tickled his nose. "*Arana, adesta,*" she whispered. It was their secret language. It meant, *I am here, friend.*

"Need to find the snake," Lucius said. "Kill the king."

Logo took his hand now. "I am afraid we are too late, master. The snake has struck. King Tarquinius lies on his death bed."

"I came as soon as I could," Demetria said. "I was visiting my family. You remember, my yearly visit? It had been a week at home and I'd been getting terrible news from the palace about a newcomer, a new haruspex. Then a snake slithered out of a pillar in the palace of the king as he was sitting in judgment over a dispute. It bit him and he fell. He is not dead—his healers have given him herbs that are counteracting the venom—but it is not known if he will live or die."

"How long...?" Lucius clutched at his side. He was lying on his own cot, under familiar bedcovers.

"You have been asleep for almost two days, master," said Logo. "I found you in the cave, managed to bring you out, but..."

"I failed!" Lucius groaned.

Demetria took his hand. "Only the gods are perfect, Lucius."

"But prodigies... I have no trouble now... none have ever..."

Now it was Logophilus' turn. "Of course you are the master of prodigies here. But this clearly was something different—something neither you nor I have seen before." He patted Lucius on the shoulder. "Rest now. There will be more to speak of when you are stronger. I just want to know one thing. We saw the bite that the serpent gave you. Did you counteract it with a grammar? You were gravely ill."

"Don't know. I made the grammar."

"What was it? If you tell me, I might be able to know how to help you recover better."

"Grammar... *venenum serpentis mago magistro... mutatom.*"

Demetria gasped.

"Changed!" Logo said. "Changed for the master mage. Certainly it must have changed in your blood!"

"How?"

"I do not know for sure. But because you used the bestower—you said 'for the master mage,' it had to be something beneficial. Something that would be a gift."

Lucius sat up with a jolt. "A gift."

"It must be. The grammar avails."

"How long will I be like this?"

"We cannot know. The venom itself was from a prodigy, so there is no telling what its properties are. They are not like any poison from this world."

Lucius sighed. "So I have a hidden gift and the king is almost dead."

"Yes, and you must heal him," Demetria said. "As soon as possible."

"The king? But he—" But what? Lucius thought back to the moment just before the serpent struck. Why would he want the king alive? He and Logophilus had spent the years since they had saved the sacred shield of Rome, the *ancile*, working on a constitution that would give power to the people of Rome and end the rule of kings forever.

But Demetria was not thinking of constitutions at the moment. "We have discovered a new enemy in the city of Rome," she explained. "A haruspex, one of the Etruscan soothsayers. This one is the great nephew of the haruspica we defeated."

"Turanquil!"

"Yes, the one who brought lightning down upon herself." said Logophilus. "Demetria—"

"I just found out about this man. His name is Lars Nepos," Demetria said.

Indeed, it had been a busy winter and spring both for the constitution and prodigies; Lucius had been occupied in keeping the otherworld spirits from causing nuisances in the city, while at the same time putting the finishing touches on the laws of Rome. All Rome still believed that Lucius Junius

Brutus, the simpleton, was living in the hills under the care of a Greek, the priest of Numa Pompilius in name only. Little did they know what he was planning for them.

Demetria continued: "I learned that this new haruspex—he is a young man, perhaps only a year older than we—has come from the capital city of the Etruscans, Veii, to take over as chief haruspex in Rome. The slaves in the palace let me know that this man is dangerous. He carries about a mirror of two metals: bronze on the face, iron in the handle and frame. Jewels are set into the frame, and the frame itself is worked with spikes. He can use the mirror for magic or for a weapon. He became angry and struck a slave with it. The slave was poisoned and died screaming in pain."

"What is this scoundrel after?" Lucius asked.

"He wants revenge for his kin. That's one thing we do know."

"And now, with the prodigy of the serpent, I think we know another thing," said Logophilus, speaking calmly and again patting Lucius on a shoulder to calm him.

Lucius, however, was feeling new strength. "What?" he said, remembering again how he had not been able to defeat the serpent. "Is it that he used the prodigy to kill the king?"

"There can be no other conclusion. It's clear he wants to get the king out of the way and rule Rome himself."

"As king?"

"Perhaps. But more likely he wishes to install someone of his own choosing and rule through him."

"Why couldn't he use Tarquin?"

Demetria now: "That's just it, Lucius. Tarquin hates him. He sent him away just a few days ago, asking him to bear a

11

letter back to the College of Haruspices. He found Lars Nepos insolent and uncontrollable. Just a day later, the serpent appeared."

"The king is our ally, Lucius," said Logophilus.

Logo was right. Lucius closed his eyes, shaken by this news but resigned. He would need to use grammar to strengthen himself and then—strangely enough—heal Tarquin.

"You will need to use darkness and stealth," Logo said. "Find a way in to the palace through grammar, and hope that Lars Nepos is not on guard."

"I can defeat him," Lucius said, balling his fist. "Maybe I should do it before I heal the king."

"Not so fast," said Logo. "The mirror is like nothing we've seen before. And if, as seems likely, he can control a snake that comes out of the Roman Spirit World, there is no telling what else he can do. He is much more dangerous than Turanquil. We must find out the limits of his power before we confront him."

"Heal Tarquin—keep the power of Rome away from Nepos for now," Demetria said. "Then we see what we can see."

"Very well," Lucius said, his purpose clear. "Let's get started."

::III::

Not many hours after the conversation with Demetria and Logo, Lucius rose up in flight with the grammarstone-filled *baculum* as his help. He would not have been able to do so except that he made a new grammar to strengthen himself and the power of Latin grammar had given his arms and legs new life.

The hair on Lucius' arms and on the back of his neck stood on end as the breeze whipped by him, as much by the cold as by the thought that Lars Nepos, this new, revenge-minded haruspex, could control a prodigy coming from the Roman spirit world. Previously, the haruspices, Etruscan seers of the future, could only anticipate what would happen and act against it. Now, it seemed, this Nepos was making the future happen, creating a new monster outside the realm of the traditional power of the Etruscans.

It was incredible.

Nevertheless, Lucius must think only on the king for now. Hopefully he was still alive; Lucius would not be able to tell until he reached the royal chamber.

Tarquinius would be guarded, certainly. He would be watched at all hours of the day and night. Lucius would have to be good with his grammar and he would have to have some luck from the gods as well.

A half-hour's flight brought Lucius over the darkened city. There was no moon, which was good for concealment, but made it more difficult to find what he was looking for, the king's residence on the Palatine Hill. Fortunately, among the few lamps burning at that time—Lucius' journey had been undertaken late, on purpose—were the ones in the bedroom of King Tarquinius.

It was a corner room, on the second floor of the palace, with windows on either side from which the lamplight emerged. Lucius alit like the god Mercury on the tiles of the roof, whispering as he did a grammar for silence on his feet. He'd learned a long time ago that a grammar of general silence would have made him unable to speak anything else, magic or not.

He lay flat on the gently-sloped roof, and peeked over the eaves. He could have easily pitched off the roof—or lost the *baculum*—if he was not careful, and he was still weak from the snakebite, so his head spun for a moment. But he pulled up his head, breathed deeply, and waited till the feeling passed.

Once he could look into the room, the sight was encouraging. There was Tarquin, clearly, covered to the face on his bed, stricken, pale, with eyes closed, but still alive. A handmaiden sat at his side, dozing. There would be guards stationed outside his door, but perhaps Lucius would not have to encounter them.

Lucius pulled back the knob of the *baculum* so that the

grammarstone chambered there fell into his hand. "*Somniom grave ancillam,*" he whispered as he threw the stone into the room. *May deep sleep be upon the handmaiden.*

The stone turned into a fine, almost invisible smoke, smelling of the spices of far away. The girl, already sleepy in the deep night, nodded further and finally slumped in her chair. She would be asleep for a long time.

Lucius chambered another stone, took it in his hand, and said, "*magus magister aerei levis,*" *May the master mage be light on the air.* He let himself roll off the roof and the air caught him as if he was swimming in water, as buoyant as a fallen leaf on the River Tiber.

The windows were wide enough for Lucius to slip through—there were no coverings to them except for fine curtains—and using the frames for handholds, he pushed into the room that now smelled of burning oil and the fragrance of sleep smoke.

With his feet still silent he released the grammar of buoyancy—*magus magister pondus quotidianom tenens* (*may the master mage have his everyday weight*)—and tiptoed quietly over to the king's bed.

King Tarquin was a strong man normally, with a heavy black beard tinged with gray. Though past forty, he still had much hair on his head as well, which gave him an air of strength and vitality when he stood before the people. His skin was dark and flushed easily and his eyes were stern, black pools of judgment.

Lucius had never liked or trusted Tarquin. He was the one who had given Lucius the name "Brutus" on the eve of Lucius' fourteenth birthday. Hardly dried from his swim across the river Tiber, Lucius had stood before the king on a warmer night than this, to claim his place in the Roman army, the privilege of any boy who had swum the Tiber before turning fourteen.

But the wish of his father, for Lucius to be a priest of Numa Pompilius, had finally won out in his heart, and Tarquin mocked him for it. Who would want to spend his life on a remote hilltop, guarding dusty scrolls that were the relics of a king whose power was long past?

Romans, Tarquin seemed to say, were of no import. They would need to follow the Etruscans if they wanted to win glory.

Now Lucius was ready to give Tarquin back his life.

"Was I such a simpleton to choose to be a priest?" Lucius whispered.

He knelt.

Tarquin's breathing was shallow. He looked so much older now; his lips were pale, his skin paler.

Lucius again retrieved a grammarstone from the *baculum*. He parted the king's lips and placed the stone on his tongue.

"*Recs sanus corpori factus*," he whispered. *May the king be made well in his body.*

The stone disappeared.

The king coughed, and sighed.

The door to the bedroom creaked.

"*Magus magister invisus!*" *May the master mage be unseen*, Lucius whispered, swiftly chambering and casting a grammarstone from the *baculum* onto the ground.

A breeze freshened, lifting the curtains and banishing the smell of the sleeping smoke.

Lucius disappeared into a kind of mist, so thin that most people would not have noticed it in the tricky lamplight.

But "most people" did not enter the room.

The door now swung open and a guard, in full armor and with a sword slung on a belt around his shoulder, held it for two others. One was a physician. Lucius could tell because he carried a bag that immediately disclosed its contents through its striking, almost stinking smell: healing herbs.

The other was a tall young man—very tall, two hands taller than Lucius himself, who was not small for a Roman. His figure was imposing, his shoulders broad and arms muscular. If he had not been dressed in the robe of a haruspex and wearing their traditional peaked cap, Lucius may not have recognized him for an Etruscan seer. He had much more the physique of an athlete or a warrior than a priest who looks into the future.

In the near dark the man's face was hard to make out, but there was no mistaking his ancestry: he had the hard mouth and eyes of Turanquil, his aunt.

But it was the mirror (the haruspex clutched it like a sword—it was half as long as the guard's own blade) that impressed Lucius the most. The frame was of polished iron, only the face itself made of bronze, and the edges of the frame were worked so that they came into points all around. At the top of the frame, a particularly sharp and barbed metal point protruded.

A weapon to be feared, Lucius reminded himself.

"The girl has fallen asleep," observed the physician in Etruscan. It was not his first language, but he spoke it well. He was most likely Greek. The king was known to have a physician as a slave.

17

The guard shook the handmaiden, who started awake.

"Forgive me!" she cried in Latin, falling to her knees.

The haruspex ignored the handmaiden. "Examine the king," he said to the physician, also in Etruscan. "The signs suggest his recovery."

The physician knelt at the king's bedside and pulled back the covers. He felt his heart, brought his face close to the king's.

The physician let out of a cry of astonishment. "Much stronger breath even than an hour ago!"

"Your herbs avail, Asclepiades," said the haruspex.

"Never this well before," said Asclepiades. It was an appropriate name: Aesculapius, as the Romans called him, was a healer of great renown who became immortal.

"Thank the gods," came the reply.

The voice of the haruspex should have been chilling to Lucius. Though what he said was simple enough, there was a menace to them underneath, a rare quality in a man of the haruspex's age. In fact, Lucius was beginning to become a bit jealous of the haruspex's strength and confidence. What was someone not much older than Lucius himself doing, lording it over people, seemingly in charge of the most important thing in Rome at that time, the life of the king?

"Lars Nepos, your mirror has told you truly," said Asclepiades, looking up. "The king will live."

Nepos. Lucius almost hissed out his name aloud. Of course it was he. But Lucius had not been anticipating a muscular giant as his opponent. It was unsettling.

"There is another thing," said Nepos. He looked about the room and his eyes stopped where Lucius was standing.

"Guard, search the room."

"My master?" The guard blurted.

"You heard me. Search the room."

"For what, my master?"

"Don't ask me questions, simpleton. Just do it."

Nepos had called the guard *Brutus*, simpleton. Was Nepos so perceptive that he could tell not only that someone was hiding in the room, but also that the hider was Lucius Junius Brutus?

Lucius had backed into a corner. Now he stepped sideways, along a wall, with his still silent feet, toward the window.

"Hey! You out there," Nepos growled. He turned to the door and beckoned for the other guard. "Go. Search the room. And cause this girl to join you."

The second guard looked just as bewildered as the first, but he pulled the handmaiden to her feet and followed the first guard, who was creeping forward, swiveling his head back and forth, looking for he knew not what.

At Nepos' command, they all went to separate corners of the room and began running their hands up and down the walls.

"What do you see, young man?" asked Asclepiades. "A ghost? A prodigy?"

Nepos brought his mirror up, as if in defense. "It may be a prodigy, but it is as real as the snake that bit the king." He spoke a few words in Etruscan. The mirror's bronze disk began to glow.

Lucius brought up his *baculum* and chambered a grammarstone. It would be heard, but he didn't care. This was the moment, he thought, when he would test the strength of

Roman magic against the strength of Etruscan mirrors.

"What was that?" Nepos barked.

"A scraping—some kind of rock or stone," Asclepiades diagnosed.

One of the guards pointed to the window. "It came from there!"

The other guard clutched at what seemed to be empty air. "It's—there's something—"

Nepos' mirror suddenly flashed. An intensely bright light beamed from it and bathed the window and curtains in white brilliance. The guards and handmaiden stumbled away and shielded their eyes. In the light, there was no doubt that whatever or whoever was hiding would be revealed.

But there was nothing—no one—there.

::IV::

"You did well, master," Logo said.

Demetria echoed him. "There was no reason to match him skill for skill at that moment. Find a better time."

"He is an annoying bully. Full of himself. He deserves to be shown that his mirror is but a plaything," Lucius said.

They were eating breakfast the next morning, flatbread warmed on Logo's cooking disk over the fire.

"It is hardly a plaything," said Logo. He squinted up at the strengthening sun. It would be a fine, cloudless day. "We do not know how much power he commands. It is something unforeseen."

"We should set out for Rome today," Lucius said. "To make sure the king is still well. And to begin to plot this Nepos' downfall."

Demetria nodded. "It is a little early for your visit to your family, but this week is good luck for traveling, according to the calendar. The Parilia festival will be held soon and many from out of town will be lodging in Rome for it."

"The festival of shepherds!" Logo exclaimed. "There will be a real stink of animals along the streets."

"And mud," Demetria added.

"Isn't there always?" Lucius said with a smile.

Demetria and Lucius decided to walk from the shrine of Numa to Rome, as it was daylight and flying by means of grammarstones would certainly be noticed. It was a walk with which by now both were long familiar. They said farewell to Logo at the stump of the crooked fig tree where Lucius had first met the faithful Greek.

"Be careful," Logo said. "And bring me word as soon as you can."

The youths walked through a brief rain shower that wetted their cloaks and petasi, wide-brimmed traveling hats, but was not strong enough to soak them. The flowers in their profusion along the trail and up and down the hillsides seemed to welcome the moisture and, after the clouds parted, everything gleamed.

Lucius' mind strayed to the beam of light that Nepos had employed. In the sliver of a moment before the mirror had flashed, Lucius had thought better of a fight and jumped from the window, speaking a grammar of buoyancy again. Would the light have revealed him, though the magic guaranteed that he would be unseen?

"You are full of silence today," Demetria said.

"Lars Nepos. He is—" Lucius broke off, could not finish.

"It is best not to worry about him now. The God of Everything will reveal what to do in good time."

Demetria had begun to refer to the God of Everything more and more often now. It had been, a long time ago, a divinity that they had sacrificed twigs and bugs too when they spoke their secret language of friendship in the thickets behind Lucius' house. But Demetria used it now as a way of reassuring herself and Lucius—a way of saying that "everything" would be all right.

"I am not worrying," Lucius said, and grimaced. "I am merely making a plan."

Demetria let him be; Lucius was grateful for it. They knew each other, knew each other's moods, almost without having to ask. A closer friend Lucius could not imagine.

In Rome preparations for the Parilia had already begun. Extra animal pens were being set up in the Forum, and altars to the god Pales, a mysterious divinity, were being raised. There would be music, revelry, and even athletic games in a few days.

But there was also much other work going on. The king had ordered the temple of Jupiter Optimus Maximus, under construction for long years, to be finished with all haste. He had also decided to dry out the low-lying ground in the space between the Palatine and Capitoline hills. Winter rains often flooded the Forum, and mud clogged the streets for most of the year. The Cloaca Maxima, a set of channels to be dug and lined with stone, with accompanying footbridges and walkways, would confine the water and drain it except in the most extraordinary of rainy times.

The building program was a source of endless conversation at the dinner Lucius attended with his family that night. The guest was Arruns Tarquinius, the son of the king and a friend of Lucius' before he had become a priest.

"The problem is," said Marcus Junius the Elder, Lucius'

father, "that the king has demanded too many Romans to work on this project. They are neglecting their farms and are threatened with losing their crops."

Arruns thought a moment before replying. "I do believe my father is employing only those at Rome who have no other work to do. Not everyone has a farm."

"Nonsense, young man. There is talk that even the shepherds will be put to work this week when they arrive for the Parilia, so that the Cloaca will remain on schedule."

"With respect, good father," Arruns began, but he was not allowed to finish.

A messenger was shown into the dining room. He had clearly been running.

"The king requests..." He stopped for a moment to catch his breath. "King Tarquinius requests the presence of Lucius Junius Brutus and the Greek Demetria daughter of Istocles at the palace immediately."

"Immediately?" Marcus the Elder's eyes narrowed. "What can be the need?"

"Good father, I do not know," said the messenger.

"I will go with you," said Arruns. "I gave word to my father that Lucius had arrived back in Rome this afternoon. Maybe he wants to welcome him personally."

Marcus the Elder's eyes met briefly with Lucius'. He had never been told of Lucius' deception, and thought, along with Junia his mother and most of the household, that he was indeed a simpleton. But there were times when, Lucius understood, there was something more than suspicion of the truth in Marcus' mind. He had one son left—Lucius—who was possibly a threat to the King Tarquin because he was his sister's son, next in line for the throne after Tarquin's sons Sextus, Arruns, and Titus. The king needed to keep on eye on this simpleton and Marcus Junius the Elder had to as well.

Lucius shook his head as he thought of the long years he had kept the secret of Brutus from his father. It did not feel right; it seemed like disrespect. But Logo had said, and Demetria had agreed, that it was the best policy for all. The fewer things people knew, the fewer they could reveal.

The way to the palace of the king was down the Capitoline hill, by the gleaming marble of the temple swathed still in scaffolding as the columns were painstakingly being raised. Then through the Forum they went, with channels laid out and piles of tufa, the native Roman stone, waiting to be squared off with the chisel and stacked in the channels. The Palatine Hill rose before them, dotted with umbrella pines, spreading oaks, and leafy cornel trees.

Arruns, puffing and nearly out of breath, said to Demetria, "We need not go so fast. Father will still be there whether we run or walk."

Lucius was grateful that Arruns was still alive. He had always been weak and was often ill, so was not considered the favorite for the kingship. That was Titus, the eldest, already an officer in the Roman army. But Arruns was a friend and both Lucius and Demetria thought he would be an ally when they gave Rome back to the people of Rome—when Etruscans would no longer rule in the city.

Demetria slowed her pace, but just a little. It was clear she wanted to know what the king was after in requesting this meeting at the dinner hour.

They were met by guards at the threshold of the palace and

quickly ushered into a room in the interior of the house on the first floor that had no windows and was lit both by candles on stands and by lamps.

Lucius had to take care not to raise his head up to the second floor, to that corner room where he had almost fought Lars Nepos. Everything depended on his playing his part well. Nepos might know the truth about him, for his aunt Turanquil had fought him openly—but had she the chance to inform her nephew about him before she perished?

They were alone in the room for very little time before Tarquin's other two sons Sextus and Titus joined them. Titus, the eldest, was clad in a ceremonial breastplate interlaced with iron ribs and skirts also in leather and iron. Sextus was similarly clad. Both resembled younger versions of their father, though Titus was bulkier, with full cheeks and stronger nose. Sextus, younger than Lucius by a year or two, still resembled a boy in some ways, though he tried to look the part of the fierce warrior prince.

Both sons greeted Arruns and eyed Lucius, clearly uncomfortable in his presence, though the curl of a smile on Sextus' face betrayed another emotion: contempt.

Tarquinius' wife Tullia, the queen of Rome, was next to enter. She was tall and thin, wearing a long linen robe and a *palla*, a kind of shawl, over her head. She was younger than Tarquin, but had the air of a grandmother, a respected woman, about her. Arruns shared her grey, searching eyes and delicate features. She took everything in silently, and paid special attention to Lucius, who only raised his head now and then, and with as vacant an expression as he could muster.

Finally, King Tarquin entered, carried on a litter-chair by

four slaves, one on each end of the two poles that slotted through the chair. Tarquinius was pale, but clear-eyed, his hair noticeably grayer than before.

"I welcome the royal family of Rome," the king said as the slaves put down the chair. His voice matched his appearance: weak, but steady, and lucid. "My children, my nephew who is inflicted with the disease of Numa Pompilius, my wife and the comfort of this short life. I speak to you by all the gods of Rome who keep the city."

This last was a signal. Everyone knew the response and said it together: "And we, who obey the gods, listen to the king."

"The snake that came from the pillar is a sign," Tarquin said. "I have asked the chief haruspex, Lars Nepos, to interpret it. He will explain it to you now."

As if on cue, Nepos swept into the room. He was wearing the pointed hat and long robe of a haruspex, and held his mirror at his side.

"What I have to say," he began, "is for your ears only. Do not disclose it, on pain of death."

::V::

Demetria gasped, seeing the haruspex for the first time, and Nepos, noticing her astonishment, puffed out his chest and allowed himself a quiet smile.

"We must first thank the skill of the king's physician and the divine will of the gods for sparing the king's life from the venom of the serpent," he said, his voice strong and commanding, and yet respectful of the king, who sat quietly nodding as he spoke. "As it was their will that he live, we see that the gods have delivered a powerful message through this ordeal."

His eyes seemed bright as embers as he spoke, though they were as dark as flint. "The snake was a Roman prodigy. There is nothing in the Etruscan spirit world that intends harm to an Etruscan king. And this is the first great sign, that there are those Romans who intend harm to the king. That is why the snake came."

Both Lucius and Demetria bristled, though they could not protest. It was Nepos who had brought the prodigy, so Logo

28

insisted, but they could not give away that knowledge.

"The snake emerged from a wooden pillar in the middle of the house, near the seat of judgment," Nepos went on. "This pillar, being in the center, supports the house of Tarquinius and therefore is a sign of the strength of the Etruscan rule. Because the snake came from the pillar, it is telling us that there is a weakness in the kingship."

Tarquinius nodded as before, though he narrowed his eyes when he heard "weakness."

As if acknowledging Tarquinius' discomfort, Nepos added, "It is not a weakness of the king's mind, heart, or dedication to Rome and the Etruscan nation and people. It is merely an indication that life does not go on forever. Someday a new king must rise. And it must be an Etruscan king."

"I have three sons," said Tarquinius. "But I only have one kingdom. So it is upon me to determine which of the three will rule and which will defend that rule. Yet I am but a man, as Lars Nepos reminds me, and it is the gods who should decide which of the three will be king. When the gods decide, the people prosper."

At this, both Titus and Sextus shifted uncomfortably; Titus brought his arms over his chest and frowned. As the eldest and already an officer, he would have the advantage over his brothers in receiving the kingship, but it was not the custom among Etruscans or Romans always to give all property to the eldest.

Sextus was a warrior like Titus, but young and without judgment, and so was not considered a likely replacement for Tarquin.

Arruns, for his part, looked bored. He screwed up his

mouth on one side. He had been part of the boys' assembly before Lucius had left for the shrine of Numa, and like Lucius he had the idea that there should be no king, but that the people of Rome should decide its fate.

"In our tradition," Nepos now said, "it is up to the haruspices to read the signs in the entrails of beasts to determine the gods' will in these matters. Romans, for their part, look to the flight of birds. But I have foreseen another thing in this mirror I carry." He brought it up briefly, as if to show everyone what he had seen. On the back of it, so Lucius and Demetria both noticed, was crafted an Etruscan griffin, a lion with eagle's wings. "The decision is of great moment. There will be great things that come of the man who takes power from King Tarquinius. It is a matter beyond sacrifices and beyond birds. We must hear the answer from the god himself. And so..." He trailed off, and gestured with his mirror at Tarquin.

"And so," Tarquin said, "I have decided to send to the sacred shrine of Delphi to ask the wisdom of Apollo, the god of future knowledge. The oracle will speak. We will know the divine will of the gods at that time."

"To Greece?" Arruns blurted. "My father, I—"

"It is a long and dangerous journey," Nepos said, his voice rising to quiet Arruns'. "But we cannot ask just anyone to make it. A messenger is not enough. He might not be loyal— he might falsify the word of Apollo. More than that, the person who asks must be worthy to approach the shrine. He must pose the question in the proper way."

"Therefore," Tarquinius said, "I have determined, with the help of the esteemed haruspex, that Titus and Arruns, my sons, shall both go on this journey."

Titus put up his hand. "My father, I cannot go. The campaign against the Rutulians is just beginning. I am needed with the army."

"Peace, my son," said Tarquinius, raising his hand.

"To respect Apollo, the eldest must go," Nepos said.

Titus fumed, but silently.

"And Arruns, you have always been wiser than your years," Tarquinius said. "You will go also, for once having heard the response of the oracle of Delphi, you will not give a false answer. You have never wished to be king, but if it is you that is chosen, Titus will not be able to say it was he. You will tell the truth."

Arruns coughed.

"Sextus will remain behind, as an assurance. He will take over command against the Rutulians, and if the gods see fit to take both Titus and Arruns to the Land of the Dead, robbing them of the light of day, there will be a son left to take my place."

Sextus glanced at Titus, who scowled.

"You see how all the king has spoken is wise and good," Nepos said.

Lucius thought, *you mean how all you have spoken is what you intend!* And what was Lars Nepos intending? He was certainly not convinced that Apollo's knowledge was greater than those of his own gods. The Etruscans did not normally hold Greek gods in such high esteem. The powers of the haruspices were always enough—in their opinion.

"When are we to depart on this journey, father?" Arruns asked.

Tarquin again raised his hand. "There is one more thing to be said. This is a matter that Nepos suggested to me and I give it my blessing.

"In addition to Titus and Arruns, there will be a third to go. Three is lucky and pleasing to the Etruscan gods, but more importantly, this person will be able to act as the final check and confirmation of the god. Lucius Junius Brutus, the simpleton, will also accompany the sons of the king."

"What?" Demetria cried. "But he is not—not involved with the kingship."

"But he is," said Nepos. "As the son of the king's sister, he is also one who could become king. That is no matter, however. What Brutus will do is listen to the oracle's response and speak it back to us when he returns. Because he is a simpleton, he will neither be able to lie nor to conceal a false response that the two sons may decide to give him. Brutus cannot deceive, so he will be the best witness of what Apollo says."

"This is nonsense. The word of the gods should be up to the haruspex," Titus grumbled. "And up to the warriors, the defense of the nation."

"My son," Tarquinius said. He held out his hand as Titus swept by him.

"It is as you wish, o my wise father," he said. He did not turn back as he left the room.

Nepos turned to Arruns. "Have you something to say?"

"You have spoken all that is well, haruspex," Arruns said. "I have nothing else."

"Sextus?"

"I will obey my father, the king of Rome."

Of course you will, Lucius thought. *If none of us come back, you are the king.*

Nepos turned to Lucius. "Brutus, son of Junia. Speak if you have sense to do so. You go on a dangerous path and you have been chosen especially because you are a simpleton. If the gods have given you your wits back, tell us. We will rejoice and find another to go in your place."

It was all Lucius could do not to cry out that yes, he had his wits and that he would do all in his power to stop whatever plan Nepos had in mind. But, like the night before, Lucius knew that Nepos was probing, trying to reveal what was unseen about Lucius and therefore take away his advantage. He might as well give up the dream of a Rome ruled by the people if he told Nepos the truth now.

"Mirror," Lucius said, and brought up his finger to point. "Beautiful."

Nepos gave another quiet, confident smile. "He is not in his right mind, as you have heard. He will go," he said. Then, turning to Lucius, his tone turned enticing. "Brutus. The mirror is indeed beautiful. Would you like to look in it, to see your soul as it truly is?"

Demetria cut in. "No one looks in the mirror of a haruspex if he values his life."

"Mirror," Lucius said. "Nepos look."

Nepos ignored his remark and instead said, "Will you go as well, handmaiden of the simpleton? It would be well. This one will need assistance."

"Of course," Demetria said.

"It is well," Arruns said. "She speaks Greek, and neither Titus nor I are fluent in it."

"Arruns, you have received the best education from a Greek teacher," said Tarquin.

"I know the poems of Homer by heart," Arruns said. "But that is an old language, not spoken by those in Greece today. It is well. She will help us."

"She will teach you on the journey," the king said. "You must ask the question yourself."

"As you wish, wise king," Demetria said.

"Now, as it is late and I am tired, we will take leave of each other. It is the beginning of the sailing season and favorable winds and lucky days are in the near future. Go back to your house, Lucius Junius Brutus and Demetria, and await orders. Soon the gods will show a clear path to the land of Apollo."

Lucius said, "Apollo. Apollo. Bow and arrow." And he mimicked shooting into the air. He hoped that the arrow of Apollo would come down upon Nepos.

Nepos laughed. "He speaks aright. It is a good omen. Apollo is shooting the birds that tell Romans false things about the future."

Someday, Lucius thought. *Someday Rome will be rid of you, Lars Nepos*. And the Etruscans.

"It is enough," said the king. "I am weary. Good night to you all."

"Good night," Lucius said. "Good night. Good night. Good night to you all."

::VI::

Demetria left the king's palace with her head so heavy with thoughts she could hardly keep it upright.

On the one hand, the idea of going to Greece, her family's homeland, filled her with excitement and awe.

On the other...

"Lars Nepos has made a well-laid plan," Lucius whispered to her as they descended the Palatine Hill.

The sun had long set by the time they left Tarquin's home, so Demetria held a torch to light their way. They approached a herd of sheep penned up on the street on their left. Their shepherd slept in a makeshift hut next to them.

"Yes," she whispered after they had passed. "Send two out of three sons on a trip to a faraway land, plus the other heir to the throne, and leave one son behind."

"And if those three should happen never to return to Rome..."

"Sextus would be king."

"Did you notice," Lucius said, holding Demetria's hand as if she was leading a simpleton home, "how Sextus himself never said a thing about the plan? Just that he would obey his father?"

"It was a prudent of him. That way he could not be called a fool."

"He has never struck me as the smartest of all the Tarquins. And that's saying something, with Titus in the family."

"Sextus is young and easily controlled."

"Controlled. That's what Lars Nepos wants. A king who can be controlled. I have no doubt he brought that snake to kill the king and begin a change in rulership immediately. I put a stop to that plan, at least for the moment."

A group of young men approached them, singing a song of Pales. They had been drinking wine and so were in high spirits.

"Lady, do you seek an escort home this evening?" One of them cried out.

"Way for Lucius Junius Brutus, the king's sister's son," she said. She was in no mood for whatever these rowdy youths had in mind.

"The simpleton?" The youth said, his eyes shining in the torchlight.

"Where are you from?" Demetria said. "Who is your father?"

"We are simple shepherds, from, from... from Parvilia," another youth said with a laugh. The name meant "little town," but there was no such place. "We worship Pales and—and—"

"Bacchus!" The third said. "Would you like wine, Lady? The house of Nonnius is close by and has drink aplenty."

Lucius pulled a pouch from the fold of his cloak.

"What does the young man show us?" said the first. "Surely a simpleton does not need silver or gold to purchase his wine?"

"I give you..." Lucius pulled a grammarstone from the pouch and tossed it at the young men, whispering as he did so, "*Timor mentibos iuvenium—magnus.*"

May fear be in the minds of the young men—great fear.

They ran away screaming, stumbling over themselves and the sleeping shepherd, who cursed as they sprinted away.

Lucius bent over and laughed.

"Why did you do that?" Demetria said angrily. "Do you want your secret to be let out?"

"It is more difficult than you know to let others make fun of me," Lucius said. "That grammar was harmless, and it got rid of those idiots."

"Let's hope it was harmless. If they do not throw themselves into the Tiber and drown, count yourself lucky."

"I will count myself lucky if they do."

Demetria said no more; when Lucius was in such a mood there was nothing helpful she could say. And it was true—maintaining the lie that he was simple was always difficult in Rome.

Lucius, for his part, said nothing on the way back to the house, which gave Demetria a moment to think again about the journey to Delphi. She had heard a few stories about Apollo the healer and bringer of plagues with his arrows. Now also he had become the god who predicts the future, and the mountain where his temple was built, a place where the whole Greek world came to ask knowledge from the immortal. What a thing to be there!

And everyone speaking Greek together, in a place where she could feel truly proud of who she was.

It was so exciting she thought of nothing else until they

were in the presence of Lucius' parents.

"Delphi!" Marcus the Elder almost yelled when told of the plans of the king and Lars Nepos. "The king is insane. Asking his sons to get on a tiny boat and sail forever. How is it possible even to get there? We must ask your father, Demetria. He is a merchant and will know."

They consulted Istocles the next day, who told them that with favorable winds it might take them a week or two. "It has been many years since I have traveled to Greece and back. But if the king orders it, you must go, Demetria." His eyes were alight with the same fire of adventure as Demetria's own heart. It was an unusual thing to see.

Demetria's mother Eodice was less eager for her to leave. "Can they not get a slave to accompany Lucius?" she asked. "It will be a dangerous passage."

"Mother, my place is at Lucius' side," Demetria said. "It is the life which the gods have chosen for me."

This quieted her mother, for she put great store in the gods' will.

"We will have to do this," Lucius said to her in a quiet moment. "Or I must attack Nepos now and defeat him."

"We know little of his true power. It would be all—or nothing."

"We must go to Logo tonight, after dark, speak to him, and retrieve the *baculum*."

Demetria nodded. Having the magic staff that augmented the power of the grammarstones would be necessary if they were to survive a journey to Delphi.

Especially if Lars Nepos had some other prodigy—or worse—in mind with which to attack them.

It took them little time flying through the night air to reach the shrine of Numa. Kaneesh the dog barked as they alit in the clearing next to Logo's hut.

Logo had been asleep when they arrived, but he roused himself quickly. And when told of the king's plans, Logo's face, lit up from below in the glow of a lamp, mirrored that of Istocles. He said eagerly, "I wish I could go along with you! It is a place of legend, Delphi. The land where Apollo slew the serpent Pytho!"

"And it is because of a snake that we travel there!" Demetria cried, eyes shining.

"I wish I could see it in my mind's eye as clearly as you," Lucius said. "But I am a Roman and Greece is far away, Logo. What's more, Nepos means to have us die before we reach there, or at least never come back to Rome."

"Yes, that is true," Logo said. "There is no doubt of it."

"Which is why I wonder if I need to fight and defeat him before he sends us on this path to our deaths," Lucius said.

"No, indeed," Logo retorted, his expression turning sober. "This is why you will need the help of Apollo to guide you. Think about it for a moment. You do not know whether your power will be enough to defeat Nepos. You do not want to try unless you know how to do it. Is that not so?"

"Absolutely. But—"

"But this is the beauty of what you must undertake. You see, Apollo is a god of special knowledge. Tarquinius wants you to go to Delphi to seek an answer to who will be the king of Rome. You, on the other hand, must go to Delphi to seek your own answer."

"How we must defeat Lars Nepos!" Demetria cried. "It's

brilliant, Logo."

Logo smiled and thanked Demetria. "This is something I have thought for a long time would have to take place. Come with me."

He would say nothing more, but led the way with the lamp out of the hut into the darkness and to the caverns of Numa. They made their way deep inside to a recess where once lay the living body of the twin master mage, Caius Litterarius, the brother of Glyph, Lucius' teacher. There was a trunk there, a small treasure chest made of wood and iron. Logo opened the lid and took out the twin staff that had been filled with gold long ago by the smiths of the Etruscan god Sethlans, so that it could no longer throw grammarstones.

"Give this as a gift to Apollo," said Logo, holding it out to Lucius. "It is the greatest thing you could ever give to immortals. The god will then give you the answer to what you seek."

"It is a great offering!" Lucius whispered, taking it. "Perhaps too great! This is the heirloom of our nation."

"But it will bind the lands of Rome and Greece together forever. And—"

He stopped in mid-sentence and stared at Lucius, who was still holding the staff.

Kaneesh, who had been lying under their feet, stood up and barked.

"What is it?" Lucius asked.

"The gold!" Demetria said. "*Venenom magistro mago mutatom!*"

Lucius still had no idea what the two Greeks could be intending.

"Quick, a mirror, Demetria," Logo said. "You have one, do

you not?"

"Do you think me vain?" she said, frowning.

Lucius was growing impatient. "What is it? My face?"

"Yes!"

Lucius spoke a grammar: *magister magus suom vultom videns.*
May the master mage see his own face.

An image appeared in the space of front of Lucius, as if a
perfect mirror had been created.

"Do you see?" Logo asked. "In your eyes!"

Lucius did see. The whites of his eyes had turned to gold.

"It is of the gods," Logo said. "The poison in your veins
has turned to gold."

Kaneesh barked again.

Logo nodded at the dog. "Yes, girl. Here. Let us see." He
took the staff from Lucius' hands, then looked in the grammar-
mirror again.

The whites of Lucius' eyes had their normal color.

They checked several times to be sure. Each time Lucius
held the gold-filled *baculum*, his eyes changed.

"Be sure to show this to the priest when you make the
offering," Logo said.

Demetria clapped her hands. "Yes! It is a sign of Lucius'
own character!"

"What are you saying, Demetria?" Lucius asked.

"On the outside, horn," Demetria explained. "It is the
material of an animal, something that has no wits. But on the
inside, gold. Pure, strong, and valuable. Your true nature. You
will be telling the priest that you are in your right mind."

Logo bowed to Demetria. "Well said."

Kaneesh whined and wagged her tail.

"And as for your own *baculum*, master, I want to show you something," Logo said. They retreated from the inner chamber to Lucius' own living area, which was nearer to the entrances of the caverns. His working *baculum* usually rested on two nails on the wall next a table where Lucius studied Latin grammar. But now it was on the table itself, next to a staff of wood slightly larger than itself.

"Look here at what I have done," Logo said. He took the two staffs, each in one hand, and held them in front of him. "I have taken a sturdy, straight limb of cornel wood and hollowed it out." He sighted down one end of the wooden staff, as if he were looking through a pipe.

Demetria took the staff as Logo offered it to her, and also sighted down it. Indeed, there was a substantial round hole in the limb that went deep into it.

"Hollowed it out? For what purpose?" Lucius asked.

Demetria had a thought. "Is the hole big enough for Lucius' *baculum*?"

"It is. I have tested it," Logo said. He gave her the staff. "Put it in the wood—like into the sheath of a sword. You will see."

"It is a wonder," said Lucius as Demetria put the *baculum* into the wood. It fit snugly, but did not stick as it slid out. What was more, the wood that would cover the stick was extremely thin, yet tough.

"Every simpleton needs a walking stick—a way to keep balance, shall we say?" Logo said. "This will be yours on the trip. And if ever you need to make a grammar that requires the *baculum*, it will be there for you."

Lucius took the invention in his hands, weighed it. "A

perfect concealment! Not much thicker than a normal walking stick would be, and feels natural."

"By Zeus, a god inspired you, Logo!" Demetria said. "You have thought of everything."

"But surely there must be a knob to affix to the top of this staff?" Lucius asked.

Logo turned to the table and picked up just such a knob. "It fits on top perfectly. I have had the time to work on it this winter."

"And now we have everything we need to go to Delphi!" Demetria said. She threw herself into Logo's arms.

"Say hello to Apollo for me when you get there!" Logo said into her ear.

"I will," she said. "And you will see us return. I swear it!"

But Lucius stood apart, examining the cornel-wood staff. "By my genius," he finally said. "I wish—"

But he never finished his sentence.

::VII::

The next two weeks were spent choosing a proper day of departure and a proper means of transport.

Both the Romans and Etruscans believed that some days were luckier than others for whatever was to be done, and travel was no exception. First, the holiday of Parilia had to be celebrated. There would be no travel during this time. Then, when a good day had been picked (they decided on the second of May, the day after the Kalends), the decision had to be made about the boat.

The Romans themselves had no warships but relied on the Etruscan navy to protect their shores. Of enemies there was no shortage: the Carthaginians from Africa, and pirates from many shores plied the waters of the Tyrrhenian Sea.

Demetria and Lucius had no discussion with the king or anyone else about a ship, but one day Istocles was summoned to the palace and returned with news.

"The king wishes his sons and Lucius to go to Delphi without an Etruscan escort," he reported when he returned. "It is to be a secret journey. And he wants us Greeks to find a merchant vessel that is swift and surely captained but will not attract undue attention."

"You will not go, will you, husband?" Eodice asked.

"No, but my son-in-law Nauarchus has just arrived from Massalia and is in Ostia now. He is perfect for the job."

"Nauarchus!" Demetria said. He had once been her betrothed, when she and Lucius were fighting to retrieve the second *baculum* from the Etruscan Land of the Dead. He was now married to Demetria's aunt Phane.

"He is the best captain I know, and loyal to the family. He will do whatever I ask of him."

All Istocles said was true—Nauarchus was an excellent choice for a voyage to Greece—but she hated the idea of exposing him to whatever dangers Lars Nepos had brewed for them.

Lucius agreed, but said, "It is a blessing from the gods that we will have another ally on our journey rather than an enemy. Nauarchus will not simply take us to some island and leave us there."

Demetria had to admit that the choice of Nauarchus to be captain showed at least that Lars Nepos wanted it to appear that the journey was one that would be finished. But it remained to be seen who else would crew the ship.

On the last day of April, Titus and Arruns Tarquinius, Lucius Junius Brutus, Demetria daughter of Istocles, plus baggage and attendants stood at a dock waiting for Nauarchus' barge to arrive from Ostia to take them to the ship. It was a brilliant, blue day with a warm breeze from the west.

Titus insisted on bringing his full armor and weapons and a shield bearer named Aulus Fufetius to help him with all of it.

Arruns had brought a whole library of scrolls to be cared for by a slave, Enetius, who could also read and write, and who would be the official secretary for Arruns' descriptions of the journey.

Demetria had brought several new gowns with her at the insistence of Eodice, for they did not know how long they would be in Delphi and what festivals there might be.

Lucius, for his part, brought his *baculum* hidden in the cornel-wood staff, and a trunk with the gold-filled *baculum* hidden underneath clothes and other gifts for the god, including a bronze statuette of Romulus and Remus, the founders of Rome, suckling at the teats of the she-wolf that raised them in the wild.

The king gave to everyone a number of silver coins they might use to buy food or lodging or perhaps to encourage pirates to let them go. All of these came from Greek cities, since neither Rome nor Etruscans used coins but paid in the form of lumps of metal called ingots.

When they arrived in Ostia, Nauarchus greeted them with joy and told them the news about Phane—she was with child again, their third, and little Nausimache was now eight years old and an expert weaver of infant wrappings.

"She will make us rich someday with her skill," said Nauarchus.

It was not until Titus and Arruns had both gone to sleep that they had a chance to speak with Nauarchus about the trip. When they had told him everything, he said one thing that made both Demetria and Lucius breathe a little easier.

"My crew are all picked men. Poseidon and Zeus willing, we will get you to Delphi and back."

Lucius patted his walking stick with the *baculum* concealed inside. "And anyone who means us harm, beware."

But at the last minute, as they were boarding the boat on the second of May under those same blue skies and fresh breezes, a new traveler arrived.

"My name is Vel Uchtave," he said, a young man prematurely bald and pale.

"Octavius," said Arruns. "You are a Roman, I think."

Uchtave shook his head, but did not deny Arruns' words out loud. He carried a mirror, but it was bronze all over, unlike Lars Nepos', and he seemed to be much less threatening.

"We will need to watch him," Lucius whispered to Demetria during a quiet moment.

In the first couple of days of sailing, they mostly watched him heave his breakfast over the side of the boat. Though the weather was fine, the motion of the waves was not familiar to all, and Uchtave had a particularly hard time with it.

Arruns, too, was none too tolerant of seafaring, though he seemed to strengthen in the fresh air once he had gotten used to the rise and fall of the deck.

Titus, for his part, said little but grumbled his way through meals. This continued on until the boat pulled into the Bay of Neapolis at the end of the second day and an Etruscan ship filled with soldiers came out to meet them.

"Ho, Vipsanius!" Titus called from the deck. "It is well! I will be with you in a moment. Aulus Fufetius, your worthless lout, gather my equipment."

"With a will, lord," said the shield-bearer.

"What is it, my brother?" Arruns said.

"These men are come to take me back to the campaign

against the Rutulians," Titus explained. "I am not going to Greece, gods or no."

"Do you not wish to discover whether Apollo intends for you to be king?" Arruns asked.

"Hang that Greek godling and all his priests and priestesses with him," said Titus. "I care nothing for Greek gods and I put my trust in this." He balled his fist and flexed his arm. "Go to Apollo for all I care. By the time you return—if you return—I will be king, or at least I will have the army needed to become king. Father is weak now. The serpent has seen to that. And someone needs to make sure there will be a strong defender of the Etruscan nation in Rome."

"But what about Lars Nepos?" Demetria asked.

"What of him? A liver-looker with a pretty mirror? I make of him the price of a piece of wool—even less! If he wishes to continue on as chief haruspex, he will look not to his livers or his mirror but to me."

All this time Uchtave had been in his accustomed place lying on the deck on a long, cushioned couch with four wooden legs. But when Titus mentioned the word "mirror," he had stood up, color returning quickly to his face. "Titus," he said, in a commanding tone. "It is the will of your father that you go to Delphi."

Everyone turned to him as if he had pulled them with a single piece of rope. He had said nothing—or nearly nothing—the entire time so far.

Titus spat over the side of the boat. "And it is my will to go on campaign against the Rutulians." He turned to Aulus, who was lowering gear overboard into Vipsanius' boat. "Mind that. Don't get it wet." Turning back to the haruspex, he spoke with a bit less bluster. "Fear not. When I have beaten them, I will return to Rome in triumph. My father will thank me I did what was best for him and for Etruria."

Uchtave brought up his mirror. "The signs point to misfortune if you do this," he said.

At these words, Titus hesitated, but only for a moment. "Should I care for your signs, caster of food into the sea?"

"I—Lars Nepos—cannot allow this."

Titus' eyes narrowed.

The mirror's face began to glow. It did not glow as brightly as that of Lars Nepos when he was searching for Lucius in the king's bedroom, but it seemed to warm and deepen on its face, until it was no longer bronze, but like a pool of water with a perfect reflection of a face.

Lars Nepos' face.

"Titus!" said Nepos in his commanding voice.

Titus shook his head and leaned forward. He could not believe what he was seeing.

"Titus, come here." The voice was as clear as if the haruspex had been standing on the deck itself.

Titus looked back over the side of the ship. Vipsanius had secured a rope ladder across the two vessels for Titus to use. Aulus was in the boat already.

"Titus!"

Titus was frightened, but he still had use of his legs. He bolted for the ladder and made it almost as far as Vipsanius' ship.

But not all the way.

Uchtave's mirror flashed, and as it did the ropes fastened to the gunwales of the ships unfastened and began to move on their own.

Lucius had his hand on the knob of his cornel-wood sheath.

Demetria put her hand over his. "No!" she urged him. "Wait!"

The ropes whirled around Titus. They quickly made knots, trussing him like a calf. He fell heavily to the deck of Nauarchus' ship. And then one of the ropes flew into the face of the mirror.

Uchtave held the mirror upright as someone—Nepos?—or something pulled Titus toward it.

"I told you," the voice of Nepos came, "to come here, Titus Tarquinius."

Titus was trembling violently. "Let me loose, haruspex," he managed, though his words were as shaky as the body from which they came.

"You shall not be let loose, not until this ship has crossed over to Greece," said Nepos. "It is the will of your father."

"My father?" Titus managed.

There was no answer. The rope fell out of the mirror, the mirror returned to its bronze face, and Titus lay on the deck, tied so tightly he could not turn over.

The boat of Vipsanius, along with Aulus Fufetius, was gone, as if it had never been there. It was possible they had rowed away in fear and had disappeared over the waves—or something worse had happened.

Uchtave said, "It is the will of my master Lars Nepos that everyone enjoy themselves tonight on shore. I will stay with the prince and give him his dinner."

Nauarchus said, "By Zeus, I have seen everything now."

"And you have seen nothing, Greek," Uchtave said. "Nor any of the rest of your sailors. And this one—" he pointed to Enetius, who was holding a scroll—"will write nothing. Lars—er, the king of Rome commands it."

Nauarchus bowed. "As you wish, o wise one."

Enetius, trembling, nodded.

Nevertheless, at dinner, which was at the table of a Greek merchant known well to Nauarchus and Istocles in the city of Neapolis, Nauarchus spoke to Demetria and Lucius when there was a quiet moment. "I thought you had defeated the Etruscans and their mirrors!" he said. He had helped them through their battle with Turanquil.

"The final reckoning is still to be made," Demetria said.

"By Hercules, it will be a great battle, much greater than those fought with spear and shield."

"And you and yours will be safe through it," said Lucius. "I promise."

::VIII::

The next morning, Lucius and Demetria found Titus untied and on deck. No one said anything to him; he looked back, scowling, toward Neapolis as the boat headed south.

Nauarchus said, "We are making good time. We will see Posidoneia, a beautiful Greek city, and then we will pass through the straits of Messina, Poseidon willing, and anchor in the city of Catania there."

"I have heard the Straits of Messina are so narrow a dove cannot fly through them without touching its wings to each of its cliffs," Demetria said. She had heard many things told by sailors hosted at Istocles' hearth fire, when she was supposed to be asleep.

"These stories are not far from the truth. But with a following wind as we have had, this dove—" he lifted his chin and swept his hand in front of him to indicate his ship—"will come through and touch no rocks at all. My helmsman Kalanemos will see to that."

The youths watched land go by to their east all that day. In the evening, they anchored in a quiet bay at a town called

Temesa. At anchor next to them lay a merchant ship with a load of copper from the mines there.

The next day it was quite windy and clouds piled up in the west. The ship's sail was taut all day and the youths tired of hearing the wind's keening and the flapping of the linen. Two hours before sunset the strait of Messina came into view. The land they had been coasting on their left took a turn to the west so that they had to turn as well. A spit of land Kalanemos called the Trident of Poseidon appeared on their right and grew wider as they approached.

"There are rocks on that side," he said. "In a storm, it would be easy to be driven on to them."

As if he had spoken it into being, the wind whipped anew at the sails and in the distance, a boiling black cloud let out a tongue of lightning.

"We are in for something," Nauarchus said. "The wind has shifted."

Kalanemos tested the direction with a wet finger. "From due west. It wants to drive us away from Catania and the Trident. But there are rocks on the other side as well!"

"Go below, my brother and sister," said Nauarchus to Lucius and Demetria. "Shortly we will see what Poseidon and Zeus are intending. I do not want you blown overboard."

The youths did go below—at first. But the wind blew harder, lightning cracked above them, and the boat reeled crazily.

"We need to go back up," Lucius said. "There must be something I can do."

Demetria nodded and began making her way to the ladder to the deck. Hard drops of rain were stinging the rungs. Soon the rain would make it difficult to see; the wind was already strong enough to pick them up in a gust and cast them feet away. What could Lucius do? Would it blow over? Or would they find themselves in the sea?

Lucius answered her thoughts by pulling out the staff from its sheath. He chambered a grammarstone and clambered up the ladder. His own thoughts were similar to Demetria's. He couldn't see what he should do, but he was certain lives were depending on a grammarstone.

They reached above decks just as a sheet of rain covered the boat. They were soaked through in a moment, but this didn't stop Demetria from seeing something that made her clutch Lucius' cloak and scream into his ear. "A rock—we're headed for it!"

It was more than a rock. It was disaster. A pointed tooth sticking straight up from the sea.

Demetria turned to see what Kalanemos might be doing to steer the ship away, but the rain blurred her vision. When she turned back, the hard gray outline of the rock was still there, but bigger.

Lucius threw the grammarstone, and his voice flew out with it: "*Lapis scopulum incutiens.*" *May the stone be crushing the crag.*

The rock flew apart in a thousand pieces and the ship passed over it a moment later.

"Well done!" Demetria yelled.

"We won't be able to see everything in our way!" Lucius yelled back. "And we'll crash on the shore before long!"

"Something else! By Athena, we have to think quickly!"

Lucius threw a stone down toward the sea. "*Navs labens aerei undas vincens.*" *May the ship be gliding on the air conquering the waves.*

With a lurch, the vessel rose. It was practically flying, but passing over the tips of the waves rather than freely soaring in the air.

"Good! Now we must change course!" Demetria said. "The rudder will no longer be in the water and land is approaching fast!"

Lucius had no time to think what Kalanemos or Nauarchus must be doing with the ship gliding on its own. And since it was gliding, that meant it was going a lot faster toward land than it would have in the sea alone.

"*O equi aelati maximi navei ligati rudentibus pellantes navem via salutis.*"

I summon very large winged horses tied on the ship by ropes pulling the ship on the way of safety.

It may have been the longest grammar he had ever perfected.

For each of the horses he expended a grammarstone, and as each grammarstone left the *baculum*, a silvery thread of rope spooled out along with the stone and at the end of it, a magnificent creature resembling Pegasus, the winged horse of Greek myth.

"By Zeus!" Demetria cried, though Lucius could hardly hear her over the wind.

There were four white horses, nearly twice as big as a horse that ran on land, all of them with harnesses of the silvery rope Lucius had summoned. They beat their wings in harmony, beautiful silver wings flecked with gold, and the ship gently rocked to the right as the ropes grew taut and the horses guided them back from the coast and into the middle of the strait.

The ship skimmed over the waves, going three and four times as fast as it would under sail or rowing power alone, and they were very nearly past the city of Catania when the ropes faded to nothing and the horses, freed from their bonds, flew into the sky, lost in the clouds.

The ship set itself down in the waves again with a sharp bang. Most held on to gunwale or oar, but all shouted as one at the shock.

The wind was still great but in the shelter of the spit known as Poseidon's Trident it was not nearly as bad.

Nauarchus gave the order to row, and Kalanemos bent his back against the rudder, steering to shore.

The storm blew by them, now a spring squall.

"Do you think anybody noticed?" Lucius asked.

"What? The horses?" Demetria asked. "I don't see how anybody couldn't."

Lucius shrugged. "It's what I thought of."

"You couldn't have made them the color of the sea, perhaps? Or invisible?"

"Demetria—"

"They were beautiful." She closed her eyes, and a picture of those gleaming wings came to her again. "I just wish—I wish we could fly to Delphi on them." She leaned into Lucius and they embraced. "Thank you."

Lucius held on to her as tight as he could, as if to will away the constant movement of the ship.

"Let's see what they saw," he said after a time.

Demetria managed a smile. "Uchtave was no doubt in his cabin, heaving up his lunch."

"No doubt."

"Hail!" Nauarchus cried out to them. "Have you two been there all this time?"

"Holding on for dear life!" Demetria called back.

"I told you to go below."

"We were thrown here by the sea."

Nauarchus did not reply. The wind whipped his cloak. Behind him, Kalanemos grunted with exertion as he held course.

"Where is Uchtave?" Demetria finally said.

"I expect he is below, where he should be."

"And Titus?"

"With Uchtave. He will not let the prince out of his sight."

"And Arruns?"

Arruns answered that question himself. "Here I am," he said.

"Where?"

He raised his hand. He was with the rowing sailors, the third bench on the left.

"Arruns! But how?"

"I thought I could be of help."

"You rowed for your life. It was a valiant deed," Demetria said.

"I don't think so. I didn't do anything, truly. Neither did these men. The storm was too strong. We all saw what happened."

"The horses?"

"The horses. Which god should we thank, Demetria?"

"Any you wish."

Arruns stared at her, then at Lucius, who was looking away at the sea, at the sun finally breaking through cloud.

Titus emerged from below decks. "Hail to you all. Have we survived on this little leaf in the Tiber?"

"Hail, Titus," Nauarchus said.

"I cannot say I have seen many storms from the sea itself," said Titus. "I am a man who prefers to stay on dry land. But this one was passing strange."

Arruns stood up from his bench, rolled his arms a couple of times. "Strange in what way, brother?"

"By Jupiter! We seemed to be flying, like Venus' doves. I know because after a time we fell back into the sea, like that." he punched the air with a fist. "The liver-looker lost his balance and hit his head."

"What? Is he all right?"

"Oh, yes. He is breathing. Not awake, yet. It was a nasty shock. I was thrown to my knees by it."

"Alive, by the gods. That is a mercy."

"Yes," said Titus. "But his luck only went so far."

"So far?" Demetria this time.

"Yes. It is a sad thing. The fall knocked his mirror from his hands. It went sliding out of the cabin, underneath the door. I know not where it is."

"Surely it is just outside the door," said Nauarchus.

"I do not think so," said Titus, then, with a low laugh, he added, "By Mars."

::IX::

Uchtave indeed had a knot on his forehead, but no one could tell whether it had been inflicted by the deck—or by Titus.

In any case, the mirror was gone.

"Most likely over the side during the storm," Lucius mused as they rowed into the harbor at Catania.

"Thrown as far as it could be," Demetria said. "And it sunk."

"Do you think Titus will attempt to escape now? Now that there is no magic rope to hold him?"

"These are Greek lands. No one who speaks Latin lives here. Few friends for Titus. He would face a long and difficult journey back."

Lucius readily agreed. In a way, he was grateful. There was something about Titus that was reassuring, despite his rebelliousness.

That night they watched the harbor turn red, then purple, then deepest blue, as the sun set behind them while they sat at table on a hilltop, grapevines growing up trellises all around them.

"It is as if the storm never happened," Arruns said.

Uchtave rubbed his forehead.

Titus said, "I am going to retire. How many more days till we reach the dwelling place of Apollo, Master Captain?"

"A week, perhaps," Nauarchus said. "Pray Poseidon for good weather."

"I am going to pray my genius I return to Rome in time to defeat the Rutulians. Apollo's response will be of no use to us if there is no city over which to be king!" And he directed a slave to lead him to his quarters.

"I am going to retire as well," said Uchtave. "And if I be strangled in my sleep tomorrow morning, you will know who to blame."

Arruns gave a short laugh. "No fear of that, haruspex. My brother is an honest man."

"I do not refer to your brother, prince."

And Uchtave was gone, like a spirit.

The remaining company, Nauarchus, Demetria, Arruns, and Lucius, all looked at each other around the table. Slaves had set up a candelabra so that their faces were limned in the light of the seething candles.

"I suppose we can speak freely?" Arruns now said.

"As you like," Demetria said.

"We all saw those flying horses carrying the ship like it was a two-wheeled chariot. The rowers saw it, the helmsman saw it. I didn't see exactly how they came to be. And I cannot rule out that a god saw fit to give us a blessing just at the right time. But I also saw Demetria and Lucius in the front of the boat. I saw Lucius pop up with his walking stick. He flicked it four times.

It was raining and I couldn't quite see. But four times he waved his stick and four horses came from nowhere."

Lucius now looked Arruns in the eye, with recognition.

"I knew it," Arruns whispered. "Not a simpleton."

"A friend," Lucius whispered back.

Arruns stood up. "Your secret," he said, "whatever it is, is safe with me. But if you should attempt to overthrow my father from the throne, I will instantly reveal you. That you are not a simpleton at all. We spoke a long time ago about a senate, an assembly that would make laws together, for Rome. I hope someday that will come true. But we all know," and here he frowned. "We know that men, once they acquire power, do not like to give it up. My father is a good man. He has made Rome an important city in the Etruscan nation. He deserves to rule as long as the gods will it."

"Arruns, we—" Demetria began.

"Now is not the time. You will tell me what you wish through your actions. And Apollo's word will tell us who is to be king after my father."

"Do you wish to be king of Rome, Arruns?"

"I do, Demetria. If Apollo wills it. And we cannot know until he speaks. And if Apollo wills it, I will be a good king and Lucius will have nothing to fear from me. Nor will the Romans. There will be a senate, someday. But not until I have ruled, and well."

Lucius extended his hand to Arruns, palm out.

Arruns shook his head. "Good rest. A week ahead of us, you say, Master Nauarchus?"

"May it be," said Nauarchus.

Arruns left, disappearing out of the candlelight.

"He is an Etruscan," Lucius said after a time. There was no little trace of bitterness in his voice.

"Every son favors his own father," Nauarchus said.

"Not all is lost," said Demetria. "Arruns is a good man. You will see."

Lucius reached out and took Demetria's hand in his. "I know."

::X::

The next days stretched out long, like a lion on a hot, cloudless afternoon. The sun made dazzles on the waves and the breeze was light, sometimes too light for sailing, so that the sailors had to row for an hour at a time. They coasted now with land on their left again, but traveling northeast instead of south, taking a safe route as close to land as possible, then briefly across the Ionian Sea to the coast of Greece.

"We are guarding precious cargo," Nauarchus said more than once. "Three princes and a Greek merchant's daughter."

Demetria laughed at this. Lucius thrilled to hear her happy.

All, even Uchtave, got more used to the rock and sway of the ship, and spirits rose in the evenings when the wine was mixed in a bowl and the sun gave over to darkness for a time. The evening chill was easily warded off wrapped in a wool fleece blanket, and the early sun always gave cheer the next morning.

Arruns continued to take his turn at the oars and he even persuaded the great general Titus to sit with him for a time.

On the fourth day out from Catania, they sighted the island of Ithaca, the home of the legendary hero Ulysses, and fishing boats from there hailed them and wished them safe passage in Greek.

As they made for the opening of the Saronic Gulf in the waning sun and another welcome from a host whom Nauarchus knew, a ship appeared on the horizon with one bank of oars.

"Who is she?" Nauarchus asked Kalanemos.

"Don't know, but they are making for us quickly," said the helmsman.

"If they are pirates, the better for us," said Titus. "I haven't had anyone to fight for days."

"By the looks of the ship, there could be two dozen fighting men aboard."

"And how many are we?" Uchtave asked.

"We are sailors, not warriors," said Nauarchus.

Lucius and Demetria exchanged glances.

"Let it not be horses this time," she advised him.

"Row hard," Nauarchus commanded. "If they wish to plunder us, they will have to work for it. We are not far from land. The Achaeans have ships out patrolling in the Gulf. Perhaps we can make it to one of them."

Kalanemos looked doubtful, but set the rudder on a course toward the north side of the Saronic Gulf.

"Let them come," said Titus. "That idiot Fufetius took almost all my equipment, but he left my sword. I can fight very well with that."

"Do you think he could stop them?" Demetria asked Arruns, speaking behind her hand.

"He would die trying," said Arruns. "He is not much more than a simpleton himself, but he is brave."

The pirate ship—for that is what it was—steadily closed on them, using half their men as rowers, and sending about a dozen up to the prow, each of them with long knives.

"Ho!" said a man who must have been the captain. The ships were not more than a grammarstone's throw away from each other. "You need not flee us! We are humble merchants seeking to make a trade with you."

Nauarchus laughed. "We shall see you in Naupactus where we may trade over a cup of wine, friend."

The captain said, "By the gods, if you will not come to us, we must come to you. And then it will not be a fair trade, I think, as you have made these rowers tired and less willing to give you a bargain."

"What is your bargain, merchant?"

"We have a mirror that you might want to retrieve." And he held up a mirror that, even from a grammarstone's throw away, looked very like Uchtave's mirror.

"Row on," Titus said. "Row on. Row to shore."

"Ask him where he found this mirror!" Uchtave told Nauarchus.

"Let me come aboard," was the pirate captain's reply. "No harm will come to you, unless you mean it for us."

Over Titus' protests, Nauarchus ordered the two ships lashed together with rope. Up close, the pirates were a bit less menacing. Underfed, with teeth missing, they may not have been a match for Titus. But their eyes were greedy, which was always dangerous.

The pirate captain said his name was Achaios, which is just

a name for a man who comes from the part of Greece they were approaching. He was young, very slender, with long limbs and a look of confidence that outstripped his situation. He brought the mirror with him along with a half-dozen greedy-eyed guards, armed with their knives.

"We are an honest band of scavengers, searching the beaches for what Poseidon has seen fit to bring from unfortunate ships," he began.

"And so you need weapons?" Kalanemos said.

"It is dangerous to be on the sea, you know that," Achaios shot back. "You have this noble warrior to protect you, do you not?"

"Is he talking about me?" Titus asked. "What is he saying?"

"We were coasting near the city of Croton some days ago. We were on the lookout for salvage, as usual."

"As usual," Nauarchus said.

"Suddenly a great fish surfaced near our boat. It was big enough to knock a hole in us if it wished. But instead it opened its mouth and spit out the mirror onto our decks. Then a voice came from the fish. 'Find the owner and you will have a great recompense. Keep it for yourself and you will have a great curse.' 'Who is this owner, Lord Fish?' I asked. 'When you see a man with a cornel-wood staff accompanied by a girl who meets your eye and does not look away, that is the boat you seek.' 'And, o Lord Fish,' I said, for I am nothing if not a clever man, 'Would it not be easier for you to seek out this boat and avoid the curse?' The fish said, 'But then you would not get your recompense.' And it disappeared to the depths of the sea, or to Hades, from whatever place it came."

Everyone stood there, stunned and at a loss for what to say.

"So," Achaios said, as no one else was speaking. "We have come for our recompense."

"We thank you for your piety to the gods," said Uchtave, who, it turned out, spoke very good Greek. "That in itself is reward enough, but in time they will give you what you deserve." And he held out his hand for the mirror.

"I think not, pointy-hat." Achaios held the mirror away as his guards drew their knives.

Titus also drew his sword, but then Achaios seemed to soften.

"Ho, my men, put away your blades." He held up the mirror again. "I think there should be a great recompense for this. It is no doubt of great value, if even the fish of the sea retrieve it."

The guards put their knives in their sheaths, and Titus did the same, though he grumbled in Etruscan that someone was likely to lose his life that day.

"By Hercules, then, tell us what you think a fair price would be," Nauarchus said.

Achaios gave each of them an appraising glance before answering. "I am not a man who knows the immortals' will, though I am clever enough. But one does need the mind of Hermes to know what the fish's message meant. I will ask very little. Only the bold girl and the boy with the staff. They will be my recompense."

"Scoundrel!" Demetria cried.

And blades were out on both sides again.

Uchtave said, "Listen to him. They outnumber us and could take all of us. He asks a reasonable price."

Nauarchus said, "Now you are the scoundrel, Etruscan."

"The pointy-hat speaks sense," said Achaios. "Why must all of you lose your freedom when only two are requested?"

"You will never take these two," said Nauarchus, shaking a fist. "Rather, take the man you think is so wise."

"He is not nearly as valuable."

Titus had now understood what was at stake. In Latin he said, "Make the mirror come to you, soothsayer. You have the power. And then there would be no more bother. You know how powerful is that cursed piece of metal."

Uchtave shook his head. "It is the mirror that has the power, not I. As long as it is not in my hands, I can do nothing with it."

Achaios said, "What is this language you speak? It comes from a far-off land, I think. Are you far from home, warrior?"

"Tell them we will fight them on land for the mirror. I and two of your best sailors, Nauarchus, can beat these men with a single prayer to Mars and a strong right hand."

The other pirates had begun clambering on top of and over the gunwales of their boat, in anticipation of action against Titus and whoever else bet their own blood. In all, Demetria had counted twenty-two, including the captain. Nauarchus had fourteen sailors, each one armed, at best, with a fish-gutting knife.

"At my order," Achaios called to his friends, his hand up.

Titus took a step forward. Six knives flew up to meet him. Twelve greedy eyes locked on to his sword hand.

"You'll not come near me, warrior," Achaios said with a triumphant grin.

"I go," said Lucius.

Everyone looked around. He was not in the circle of those

speaking, so all had to turn.

Lucius was leaning on his staff with both hands, one hand on the knob.

"What does he say, the one with the staff?" Achaios cried.

"I go," Lucius said, louder. "I go." And he pointed to the pirate ship. "Ride boat with friends."

"What does he say?"

"He is a fool, an imbecile. You need not listen to him," Nauarchus said.

Lucius shuffled forward, using the staff to help him. "I go," he said.

"Demetria, accompany him," Uchtave said in Latin. "He is making a good decision, for the first time since his mind went."

"A fool? This one is a fool?" Achaios looked Lucius up and down.

"Give me the mirror. He says he wishes to go with you," Uchtave said.

Lucius was now in the circle of the parley. "I go with you," he said, pointing at Achaios.

"I do not want a fool in my ship," said Achaios. "That is a curse as bad as this mirror."

"Go, Demetria," whispered Uchtave, still in Latin. "As soon as the mirror is in my hands, they will be no more."

Demetria hissed back, "And I can trust a haruspex? I think not."

Uchtave said to Achaios, "The mirror. They are yours."

"No, they are not," Nauarchus said.

"Beautiful mirror," Lucius was saying. "Pretty, pretty." He reached for it.

One of the pirates raised a knife. Titus raised his sword.

And then Achaios said "oof," doubled up and fell to the deck. The mirror clattered to his side.

Then, chaos.

Titus yelled and attacked. Two pirates found themselves with gashes on their arms before they were able to bring down a knife. A third was stabbed through the liver.

Demetria dived for the mirror along with Uchtave. She was there first and had her hand on the handle as Uchtave fell on her and clutched for it.

Then Uchtave got the second hit on the head of the journey.

"There's for you, Etruscan!" Demetria screamed, and then screamed with pain. The handle of the mirror had burned her hands. She let it go.

Nauarchus took a pirate by his shirt and threw him overboard. He tried with a second, but the man had no shirt and was stronger than the first. He slashed at Nauarchus and would've hit him except for Kalanemos, whose fist found the man's face.

Sixteen pirates stormed onto the ship and met fourteen sailors, all of them yelling like madmen.

Lucius was rolling on the ground with Achaios. He had used the butt of the staff to hit him in the stomach and knock the wind out of him. Then he took a grammarstone, one he had put in his hand as soon as the parley began, and wedged it between Achaios' teeth.

"*magister piratarum piscs magnus factus, loquens.*"
May the master of the pirates have become a great talking fish.

Achaios may have been able to spit out that grammarstone

and stopped the grammar from being perfected if he'd had enough breath to do so. But as his stomach was currently tied in a perfect knot from Lucius' staff blow, he was about as able to take in air as a fish would have been.

Which made Lucius' grammar as fit as it could have been.

Achaios went through a swift transformation. His legs and arms, so long, glued themselves to his body, which lengthened out even more, and became fins and tail. His skin turned green, mottled with black dots. His nose and mouth became more prominent; his eyes lost their whites. Instead of a black beard, a single whisker protruded from his fishy chin.

Lucius could no longer hold him. He flopped and fought, and from his mouth came a single word.

"CURSED!"

It was a fishy bellow, almost not a word, but it was quite loud enough for everyone to stop fighting.

"It can't be!" Nauarchus managed.

"But it can!" Arruns said.

"By Mars, Jupiter, and Minerva!" blurted Titus.

The fish flopped, rolled, bellowed CURSED again, turned end over end.

Right for Demetria.

Who rolled away just in time.

The fish instead landed directly on Uchtave, writhing and snapping.

Demetria thought at first to find a weapon and saw that the only thing close to her was the mirror. So she pivoted and used her unburned hand to clutch it.

"Take this cursed thing then!" she screamed, and thrust it deep into the mouth of the Achaios-fish.

D.W. FRAUENFELDER

The pain may have been worse this time.

What had been Achaios wriggled in agony and with one great, last effort, tipped itself upright and into the sea.

The splash sprayed onto both ships.

And then the pirates leapt for their own boat, screaming and yelling that they had come across a demon ship.

Titus did not pursue, and held the other sailors back, instead cutting the lines that held the two ships together.

It was taken as a favor. The pirates rowed for their lives.

I guess, Lucius said to himself as he lay out of breath on the deck, *two talking fish in one week is enough for anyone.*

::XI::

"Who's hurt?" Nauarchus asked.

Demetria was. She showed them burns in the shape of a mirror handle on both hands.

A couple of sailors had nicks on their wrists and another had been stabbed in the thigh, but all those wounds would mend.

"We will anoint your hands, Demetria," Nauarchus said, "and give thanks to the gods for mercy. The fish—the mirror—and where is Achaios?"

Lucius struggled to his feet. "Big fish. Magic mirror. Beautiful mirror."

"Didn't that fish jump into the boat and swallow that scoundrel?" Titus said. "I couldn't tell. I was fighting."

"It happened so fast," Demetria said.

"Where is the mirror?" Kalanemos asked.

"Didn't you see?" Arruns said. "It was Demetria. She—"

And then they all saw Uchtave at the same time.

He was lying on the deck, face down.

Everyone crowded round him and Nauarchus knelt. He rolled him over onto his back. He was limp. He had bled from ears, nose and mouth.

Nauarchus put his hand underneath Uchtave's nose to feel for breath.

There was none.

He looked up and shook his head.

Demetria gasped and let out a sob. Then she caught Lucius' eye. Could a grammarstone be used to bring someone back to life again? They'd never tried it. And did they want to? Uchtave had been the one who'd wanted to get rid of Demetria and Lucius on that pirate ship—abandon to them to whatever greedy men wanted to do with them: slavery at the very least.

"The fish hit him—instead of me," Demetria managed.

"And you threw that mirror into the fish's throat," Arruns said.

"It was all I could do to—"

"She was defending herself," said Nauarchus.

Titus said, "We must bring him to shore and bury him. He deserves that at least. But I am not sad to see him gone. Those liver-lookers and that mirror have been nothing but trouble from the start."

Demetria sought a quiet moment with Lucius as soon as she could.

"Achaios. The grammar. Were you hurt?"

"No," he said. "I am fine. We will heal your hands tonight."

"And Uchtave? Could we...?"

"His spirit has flown to the Land of the Dead," he told her. "We rob the gods of their due if we try to bring it back now. Uchtave alive again will be a curse much worse than that of the mirror alone."

Demetria nodded. It was true. She thought how, some four years ago, she and Lucius had gone to the Etruscan Land of the Dead in order to retrieve the very *baculum* that was now encased in cornel-wood. There they had been able to retrieve the staff from the goddess Vanth. But that staff was not hers. Hers were the spirits, the ghosts, the great family of the dead who made up a kind of pile of treasure in the deepest recesses of the earth.

Uchtave had joined all of them.

But it was still in Demetria's mind. If ever her father, or her mother—or Lucius—died, to be able to bring them back again would be the greatest gift. How could it be a curse? Asclepius, the healer who was Apollo's son, was skilled enough to raise the dead, and he had come to a bad end.

Demetria said a prayer to the God of Everything for the health of all their company.

They headed for Naupactus on the north side of the Saronic Gulf, an important port, where Nauarchus found lodging. They asked the father of the guesthouse about a place to bury Uchtave, and they lay him to rest the next day, on a little rise overlooking the blue sea.

"Well, brother," said Arruns as they walked down to the town under a warm sun, "Both the mirror and the Etruscan are gone. I suppose you can try to find a merchant going back to Rome. You won't have lost much time to the campaign against the Rutulians."

Titus grunted. "I have thought much on that, brother. But all this journey has been passing strange and I find myself with a debt."

"A debt?" Nauarchus asked.

"Yes, by Mars. As near as I can tell, it is the mirror that summoned the fish that saved us from a worse fate. Whether we would have beaten the pirates or not, only Jupiter can tell. But we would have much worse wounds than we do have, or I am not a fighting man. So Uchtave and his mirror, strangely enough, have made it that I must repay them. And I will do that by going to the god's home with you. It's what he would have wanted."

Demetria said, "You are an honorable warrior, Titus."

"Besides," Titus went on, "I can tell that all of you need me. That mirror is still in the fish's belly and it may return with more pirates. A strong sword arm to rally these sailors is the thing for that."

"Titus strong. Sword strong," said Lucius.

"This one has more sense than all of you know," Titus said with a short laugh.

"Oh, we know," said Arruns out of the corner of his mouth.

Titus would always say that the fish must have jumped into the boat and swallowed Achaios through some magic of the mirror. Arruns never ventured a guess and Nauarchus and Demetria allowed Titus' idea to spread among the men.

The next day was an easy sail to the town of Cirrha, the harbor town that led up to Delphi in the nearby mountains. It was a bustling place, full of shipbuilders and pilgrims to the shrine, and so had in it many houses catering to those who were asking Apollo's advice.

The guesthouse owner, a portly, balding man who welcomed the sight of Neapolitan coins, calling them "the most honest" of the weights of the towns of Greece, asked them while they ate where they were from.

"Rome," said Demetria. "Have you heard of it?"

"I have not," replied the man. "And that is saying something. I have seen Greeks from all over the world in my house. From Neapolis, yes, and as far as Massalia, which is where you are from, captain, and indeed from Emporiae which is even farther north and west. But never from a place called Rome."

"It is not Greek," said Nauarchus. "It is Etruscan."

"Rome. Roman," Lucius put in.

"Yes, I'm so sorry, Lucius Junius. Rome is Roman."

The owner laughed out loud. "That is like saying Cirrha is Cirrhan."

"Someday you might know more of Rome," said Demetria.

"Etruscans I know. They come here from time to time. But none to the shrine. They have their own gods, I think."

"And the Romans have theirs," said Demetria. "But they respect the Greek gods and the power of Apollo."

"Will you be asking a question? You had better get in line quickly. Or be prepared to wait."

Demetria leaned forward. "Oh? We would return to Rome as soon as possible. This one is a warrior who wishes to protect the city against an enemy."

The owner looked Titus up and down. "You have the look of a hero. He does not speak Greek then, I suppose? But I think you will be waiting a long time. Strange. Greeks leading Etruscans named Romans to ask a question of Apollo. But Zeus brings many strange things to light that you would not think of, eh, captain?" He patted Nauarchus on the shoulder.

"Yes," said Nauarchus. "Many strange things."

Later, after Titus had gone to bed, Lucius and Demetria brought Arruns and Nauarchus together in a courtyard under spreading oak trees.

"This loose-tongued host is sure to spread the word about us," said Lucius. "At sea and in guesthouses where Nauarchus had friends, it was easy to keep the secret that there were princes in a small merchant boat. But now we cannot know what people will think or do. As he said, there are Greeks from all over, and we do not know how many will come honestly to seek an answer from Apollo and how many come for their own gain."

"But is it not so that the power of your staff is enough to ward them all off?" Arruns said.

"Lucius can fight those he sees, when he is awake," Demetria said. "But how many thieves or kidnappers do their work in the open?"

"It was always a dangerous business," said Nauarchus. "But if, like this host, no one knows Rome or cares, you can mix among all this crowd without being noticed."

"We?" Demetria said. "And not you as well?"

"I will stay here, with my ship."

"But we need you. We need everyone who has made the journey."

Nauarchus smiled and took Demetria's hand. "You are clearly not made to be the master of a ship. I do not leave my place with it. I will send sailors with you, as warnings to bandits. But Titus will be a good bodyguard, I think."

"So be it," Arruns said. "Demetria, you will be the one who speaks with the authorities. You will ask the question."

Lucius nodded. "You are the Greek speaker. And you are the wisest among us."

Arruns added, "We will attract less attention if we keep our mouths shut. No one speaks Latin except Romans."

"Other foreigners must come to the shrine," Demetria said. "It is famous all over the world. How do you know they will not understand you? Your father asked you to speak, as you well know."

"We will know how unusual we are when we arrive," said Arruns.

"We will simply need to be on our guard," said Lucius. "I must keep my secret." And here he looked at Arruns.

"Do not worry, Lucius Junius Brutus," said Arruns. "Let us know the wisdom of Apollo. Perhaps then we will be able to tell what to do."

"Yes," said Demetria. "Exactly."

::XII::

Nauarchus hired donkeys and a guide for the ride up the mountain from Cirrha to Delphi. It was a winding, switchback trail, a sunrise to sunset climb. The mountain itself seemed hundreds of miles away, lost in a reddish haze. In between, hills covered with olive trees and meadows of dry grass, food for sheep and goats.

A dozen other pilgrims went in the same train, some riding side-saddle on their donkey, some walking alongside with baggage laid over the donkey's flanks.

"Speak to my cousin Tragopagus when you reach the shrine. He will have a place for you to lay your heads," said the Cirrhan innkeeper.

"Whatever happens, send someone back to give us news," said Nauarchus. "My Phane awaits in Massalia and I would return to her this year."

Demetria threw her arms around Nauarchus. "You are a valiant man. We will be back soon, if my prayers are answered."

"For you, they always will be," Nauarchus said.

Demetria, Lucius, and Arruns rode while Titus, sword at his side, walked and led three sailors. He could be heard speaking with them as the donkeys, copper bells around their necks chiming, began their walk. "How many miles uphill? Fifteen? Nothing. I make of that less than the price of a tuft of wool."

The sailors laughed, though Latin was not their first language. Titus had that effect on people.

It was a fine day—it would not be too hot, and a recent rain had settled the dust. For several miles the path ran relatively flat and straight, now and then under the shade of an olive tree, though always sloping up, and toward the mountain that seemed to jut directly out of that plain.

Their guide, a Cirrhan named Dromopontes, told the story that the Titans, defeated by Zeus once upon a time and confined under the earth, had attempted to break out of their prison by pushing up this mountain.

"These Greeks have many stories," said Titus after one of the sailors translated for him.

"Father, since you know, I would ask you what we must do to have the priests of Apollo answer the question for us," Demetria asked Dromophontes.

"Priests?" Dromophontes gave her a smile. "It is not priests who give the answer. It is Apollo."

"Of course, but—"

"But since you seem to lack knowledge and I am one who has it, I will tell you this. It is Apollo who speaks, but it is not the priests who say the words. It is the priestess."

"Priestess?"

"Yes. She is the Pythia. She is not unlike you, a maiden loyal to the god and with a good head on her shoulders. She is the one who goes into the depths of the temple, where the spirit of the god overcomes her. She then speaks the answer to the priests, who record it. It is all written, you know, with letters. There is much grammar there in the temple. That way everyone can know what the god said and no one is unsure."

Demetria gave a sidelong glance to Lucius, who was doing his best to seem a simpleton.

"The answers of the god—these are called oracles, if you do not already know—are of the utmost importance. Wars are fought, kingdoms lost and won, by those who have heard the oracle. Of course, the answers are not so easily gotten."

"No?"

The clinking of the donkey bells punctuated Dromophontes' answer. "No, indeed, my young maiden. Every oracle is given in the form of a poem, two lines of verse, in the manner of our Homer, the great poet who sang of Achilles and Odysseus. It is never a plain 'yes' or 'no' that comes from the mouth of the god. No, the knowledge of the gods is not plain and it is hard for a human being to know the full meaning. But a wise person can see it, if the gods allow."

"It is well," said Demetria, though she wanted to ask for an example of these two lines of verse of which the guide spoke.

"Do you come from far off?" Dromophontes asked. "The owner of the animals, Oinophon, told me you paid in good Neapolitan silver. Newly minted coin, full weight. Is there some great doing in the west, where the sun sets? We have had many come from the islands and the colonies. And there are many athletes who come for the games, from Syracuse, Messana, Catania. They are tall and strong, fast runners. Just last year a man came from Himera who was rumored to be the fastest sprinter ever seen in the western lands. He would have been the winner in an early heat here, but he tripped and broke his ankle. Some say a stone was thrown in his way..."

Dromophontes carried on his story like the flowing Tiber, forgetting his original question about from where Demetria and her company had come.

Demetria was grateful. The less people knew about them, the better, the way she saw it.

But what Dromophontes had told her had concerned her. Was it only the grand of Greece who were allowed to ask questions? How should she approach? What should she say? And the priestess—the Pythia—what was she like? Dromophontes had said she was "like" Demetria, loyal and with a good head on her shoulders. Did he mean that in other ways? Was the Pythia Demetria's age? Would they be able to speak together about what it was like to be the servant of Apollo?

These thoughts occupied Demetria all the way to the base of the hills, where the path began to rise steeply, and in long switchbacks. No longer were they among olive groves. Instead, outcrops of rock met them, tufts of grass, and hardy oak trees and thorn bushes. The path was rocky, as well, and in places the soil had washed out from winter rains. Here, the company had to pick their way over stones smoothed by the hooves of many donkeys and feet of many pilgrims.

In places, there would be a simple stone bridge over a ditch. Demetria learned to be grateful for these, for it meant faster and easier going. The sun was already well overhead and the sea, sparkling with the sun as if laid with new Neapolitan silver coins, still seemed so close, and the top of the mountain far away.

"Keep it up, lads," Titus said, face shiny with sweat. "Dinner and dancing girls on the mountain tonight."

Dromophontes said out of the corner of his mouth to Demetria, "Does your bodyguard speak Greek? This tongue he speaks sounds like the bellow of a cow. But then, barbarians can be fierce warriors, is it not so?"

"It is so," said Demetria, and smiled to herself.

"Of course, no one can handle a spear and shield as well as a Greek. When I was a younger man, we Cirrhans fought the men from Naupactus. I stood in the forefront of battle, with the other hoplites. Five times we beat them back, but then..."

Arruns rode up next to her. "I think my Greek is getting better. Just listening to this tale spinner, I have learned much."

"Maybe you wish to ask the question of the Pythia?"

Arruns laughed out loud.

The sun was lighting the western horizon when they finally gained the summit of the last hill. Clouds had come over, so that the sunset draped a red tapestry over the mountains.

"And so Helios takes to bed," Dromophontes said. "Where did you say you were to lodge tonight?"

"We were told to look for Tragopagus' house," said Demetria.

"He should have a place for you. But you must know, it will not be like the guesthouses of the men that come from Athens and Thebes. From where did you say you came?"

"Rome," Demetria said.

"Rohhhm? Is that in the land of the sunset? Near Neapolis?"

"Yes. Somewhat near."

"Well, Tragopagus will be happy to give you hospitality. He knows that Zeus often walks on this earth in disguise."

Tragopagus, a lively gray-bearded man whose belly told a story of years of feasting, was happy to give them hospitality, though it would have to be outside that night in his courtyard. "The house is full of pilgrims," he said. "The god has just given his last set of answers for the month. They will be leaving tomorrow and you can have their rooms."

"Last set of answers?" Demetria asked.

"Yes! The next set will be upon the waxing of the moon. "But you knew that, I suppose?"

Demetria decided not to answer that question, but to ask another of her own. "How long will we have to wait for an answer?"

"If you put your name on the list, you will be among the first of the next set. In three weeks' time, they should be able to speak to the god. In the meantime, there will be much to do. A troupe of players will sing holy songs to Apollo, called the Paean, for a week in the theater, every night. And of course there will be games."

"Do you mean to say that the Pythia does not come daily to her temple to consult the oracle?"

"By no means, daughter. Perhaps twice a month, all at one time. The god is not to be rushed in bringing his answer. You may ask it in three weeks, and then in another three weeks you might know."

Demetria thought hard. "But..."

"Yes?"

"May we present a gift to the god? May we do it beforehand, while we are waiting for the time of questioning?"

Tragopagus grinned and winked at her. "I see you have been speaking to the right people. Of course you may present a gift to the god. I presume you will be using Neapolitan silver as the gift?"

"We could, but we have a greater one than coins."

"Do you wish to build a treasury? That is something that must be arranged and approved."

"No. It is really a gift for the priestess's eyes only."

Now the light drained from Tragopagus' eyes. "You might have some more trouble there. Most of the time the gift is given to the priest of the storehouse, Apollodorus."

"By the god, I would speak with him then," Demetria said.

"As you wish, my daughter. I can send a messenger with your request tomorrow. But some good Neapolitan silver might help to speed him on his way and Apollodorus look favorably upon you."

Demetria was beginning to see how Delphi worked. Arruns and Titus were summoned, who gave her enough coins to satisfy Tragopagus.

"And take one for yourself, greed-guts," Titus said. He pointed to the coin and then to the Greek.

"You look with favor upon my house, warrior," Tragopagus said, bowing.

"Maybe it will get him to serve us better wine," Titus said. "What he has given us so far is not half as good as what we Etruscans make."

The men, as Tragopagus said, slept in the courtyard that night, under a grape arbor and wool fleeces, while Demetria had a cot set up for her in Tragopagus' daughters' quarters.

"You are very important to be speaking for yourself to our

father," one of them said as they lay down that night.

"We come from a land where not all speak Greek," Demetria said.

"What a shame! For you to be among such barbarians! It must be so tiresome not to live among your own people."

"I love the land where I live. It is home."

"You have traveled so far! Were there pirates?"

"There were pirates."

"Did Dionysus come and save you, and turn the pirates into dolphins?"

All the girls giggled.

"We just had this story told in the theater in the last festival. The masks of the pirates were so frightening—and then the ones when they became dolphins. And the dancing."

Demetria fell asleep to the chatter of the daughters. Her last thought was of Uchtave and the pirate turned into a fish with a mirror in its throat.

That, truly, would be a story for a theater, she thought.

.

::XIII::

The next morning it was easier to see the shape and setting of Apollo's chosen home. The town was built on an outcropping of the rust-red mountain which reared up vertically with sharp crags, the nests of eagles and hawks. The houses of Delphi, most with straw roofs, the better ones with tiled, were dwarfed next to the face of the cliff.

In the valley below—a long way below—a stream wended its way through dense forest. Now and then an olive grove had been cut into the wilderness, but mostly the country was empty of people and cultivation.

"I feel as if I am a baby bird in a nest up here," Lucius said as they looked out from the Tragopagus' courtyard. His eyes followed the stream through its little valley, out onto the plain of Cirrha, and in the distance, the town and the blue water.

"We are but mortals, and the gods are..." Demetria said. It was a line of poetry she had learned, but she had forgotten the last word. Or at least, there was no word in Latin that she remembered to translate it.

"Invincible," Lucius supplied. "I can see why the people

around here say the Titans pushed up the mountain. Only a god could have made this place."

"Do you have the gold *baculum*?"

"Yes." Lucius bent over and waggled his head, the way he did to indicate he was a simpleton and no danger to anyone. "It is slung over my back, under my tunic, and my cloak covers that."

"Good. Let's go, then."

Arruns and Titus came with them, dressed in their finest togas. Demetria herself had a good linen dress packed by her mother, and a Roman *palla* to wear over her head. She had convinced the princes to let Lucius come along, and wearing his cloak rather than a toga. They had little choice but to say yes, as Arruns still maintained that Demetria was the one to speak for them. They would never get their question answered without her willingness to do so.

The walk toward the shrine itself was downhill, paved, with stone steps and pathways. They passed first a spring, called Castalia, where they were advised by attendants to wash, to purify themselves. A stone gateway was next, manned by soldiers that came from something called the Amphictyonic League, a group of cities that guarded major sanctuaries of Greece and kept them open to all.

"What is this clothing?" One of the soldiers said as they passed by. He pointed to their togas. "I hope you did not walk far in all those folds."

The other barred their way with his spear, though not with the point. He held the shaft across the gate.

Demetria said, "It is the traditional garb of the people of Rome."

Like the others who had heard the name, the soldier who had spoken first tried it on his tongue and found it had an unfamiliar taste. "Do you speak, maiden? What about these men?"

Arruns said, "My Greek. Not so good. She speak for us."

The soldier seemed amused, but he did not move his spear. "So this Rohhm is not a Greek city. Why are you here?"

"We come to meet the priest of the storehouse, Apollodorus."

The soldiers exchanged glances. "You have a gift for the god, then?"

"We would pass, brothers," Demetria said.

"There is a tax. One piece of silver for each person."

"One piece each? A rich price to pass through a gate!"

"But you have a rich gift for the one who shoots far."

Titus said, "Are they asking for money, Demetria? Give them a slap in the face and let us be on our way."

"The large one speaks a barbarian tongue," said the soldier, and laughed. "It is like an ox was taught to speak Cretan."

His partner laughed as well, not at all in a good-natured way.

Titus stepped forward, his mouth set and nostrils flaring. He looked a bit ridiculous in his toga rather than in leather cuirass and with a sword-belt slung over his shoulder, but there was no doubt of his strong forearms as he rolled up his sleeves and balled his fists.

"Back, blanket-wearer," the first soldier said. "Unless you want to taste the tip of my spear."

Lucius was thinking hard. He had a grammarstone in his hand. He didn't want to scare off the soldiers as he had the drunken shepherds in Rome. What could he do that would not attract attention?

"They want silver for themselves," Demetria told Arruns.

"But these others are going in unmolested," Arruns said.

It was true. Other Greeks, dressed for work inside the gates, or as pilgrims, walked by without greeting the soldiers or they them.

"We can go back to the house and get money," Arruns said.

"Never, not to these lackeys," Titus said over his shoulder.

Both of the guards held their spears tighter, their eyes on Titus.

Demetria said, "Please. Tragopagus the host of travelers sent to Apollodorus this morning. He is waiting for us."

"Apollo, great god," Lucius said in Greek. Then, kneeling, he rolled a grammarstone out from his palm—like a child would a shooter marble—and whispered, "*O sagitta terram Apollinis.*" *I summon an arrow against the ground of Apollo.*

So it was. An arrow flew from the sky and struck a paving stone on the other side of the gateway where the stone had stopped. It went in, blade first, and its tail vibrated so that everyone—passersby, everyone—gasped as one.

"You see!" Arruns said, once he had gathered the nerve and enough Greek. "Apollo is angry! Let us go!"

The guards looked up at the sky, then down at the arrow. "Which one of you shot that?" the first said.

"Apollo shoots," Arruns said.

Demetria frowned.

"Who was it?" the guard sounded scared, but much angrier than before. "Who shot?"

Titus put his hand in the fold of his toga.

The soldiers brought up their spears.

"In the name of the oracle."

Someone had stepped out in front of the arrow. He was older, bearded, with a carefully shaved head, and dressed in a robe that fell all the way past his feet. On his head, a bronze circlet engraved with letters that held the cowl of his robe in place.

"Apollodorus!" the guards said.

"You hinder the pilgrims, men," said Apollodorus. "It is not proper."

"Yes, father."

Apollodorus motioned to the Romans. "Visitors from far-off barbarian lands? Come with me."

Lucius left the arrow in the street. He didn't want to give the impression that it was he who was responsible for it. But he had to admit it was possible everyone already knew.

"Thank you, father," Demetria was saying. "We do not have the tax for entry."

"Tax?" Apollodorus harrumphed. "What were they attempting to charge you?"

"A silver coin."

Another harrumph. "We will have them changed out for a fresh set of guards. We have been having problems with the Thebans this year. They send their worst warriors, thinking they have to keep the good ones back for their wars. But it is true that guard duty at Delphi can become a bit... dull, shall we say? That arrow certainly livened things up."

"I don't know where it came from," Demetria lied.

Apollodorus' brow furrowed, but he said, "Do not trouble yourself over it. Tell me of these men here."

"This is Titus Tarquinius, and his brother Arruns. We come with greetings from the king of Rome, Lucius Tarquinius."

Apollodorus bowed to the both of them and continued walking, then turned and said in Latin, "Princes of Rome?"

"Yes, father," said Arruns.

"Yes, father," Titus said, after Arruns glared at him.

"It will be a great land someday."

"How do you know, father?" Arruns asked.

"We know because Apollo knows. Of course we know."

Arruns gave Lucius and Demetria a look: not one of surprise, exactly, but it was clear he was pleased. "Apollo speaks Latin, then, as well father?"

"Apollo teaches his priests all things necessary for his worship and his glory."

He had been leading them through a crowded area of shops—of people selling all manner of things, including live animals, but mainly, it seemed, small statuettes in ceramic or bronze of Apollo. Now, they stepped up a short stone staircase and on to another level, higher, where the street was lined with small temple-like buildings.

Apollodorus continued in Latin. "The treasuries," he said, pointing. "Beautiful, are they not?"

They were. They were not like houses or temples, more like rooms in a house, but much more elaborate. Made of chiseled stone, with marble accents around the doors. Marble sculptures adorned the edges of the roofs and flanked their entrances. Griffins, gods, young men stepping forward as if to receive the crown of the victor in the games, young women holding flowers just about to blossom.

"A wonder," Titus was heard to say, and Arruns repeated

the word in Greek.

"Wait," Apollodorus said, nodding at Arruns. "You shall see a greater one."

The path switched back again, going up, always up. After the long line of treasuries, the grand temple of Apollo finally came into view. Its columns were the heaviest Demetria and Lucius had ever seen, much thicker than those ones that Tarquin had ordered for the temple of Jupiter Optimus Maximus.

Demetria said, "The columns... rise like the mountain."

"Precisely," said Apollodorus.

The columns supported frames of stone with statues placed in them; above those was the roof with its triangular niche under the eaves. There were the most beautiful, lifelike statues of Apollo in a chariot flanked by young men on his left and young women on his right. Animals also were carved there: lions, bulls, stags.

In front of the temple, an altar, an upraised stone table.

The Romans were not the only ones admiring the temple. There might have been two dozen or more people simply staring up at it.

"This way," said Apollodorus. He led them along the side of the temple, past rows of the mountainous columns. Behind the temple stood a wall, with a gate, and another soldier.

"Greetings, Philostratus," said Apollodorus in Greek.

The soldier let them by without a word.

Titus shook his head.

Inside the gate there was a courtyard with a well, flowering bushes and trees, and a great laurel tree that gave shade to it all. Behind that, a two-story house with a tiled roof, which they entered by a small door next to the tree.

The house itself was a maze of hallways and doors, but when they entered what must have been Apollodorus' office, a ray of sunshine almost blinded them. The office had a balcony of sorts that overlooked the valley. Wooden posts divided the room proper from the balcony, and floor-to-ceiling shutters, on hinges attached to the posts, were thrown open to let in the sun and a fresh breeze.

"Extraordinary, is it not?" Apollodorus lifted his hand toward the view. "Look. Apollo has given us a great gift of farseeing."

Apollodorus let them drink in the sight, summoning a slave who brought stools for all to sit on; another brought cups of wine. He also summoned a slave for writing anything down that was necessary, and finally he sat down at his own desk of carved wood, on a chair with a wicker back.

"Tragopagus tells me," he said, "that you have a gift for the god."

"Yes," said Demetria. "But it is truly for the eyes of the priestess only."

"Is it so?"

"We beg your pardon, father. We told this to Tragopagus and he said you would be the one who might help us meet her."

"No one sees the Pythia, as a rule. It is almost as if one is approaching the god himself."

"Well, if we show you the gift, might you take it to her? You must understand, what we are about to give is a sacred object of our land."

Arruns cleared his throat. "You have never spoken to us

what this gift is, Demetria."

"It was better that fewer people knew than more."

"What is it, young maiden?" Apollodorus asked. His tone had changed. He was almost whispering. "Apollo has not told me of such a sacred object."

Demetria turned to Lucius, who took off his cloak and pulled the *baculum* out from behind his shirt. It was wrapped in cloth and tied tightly with twine.

"What?" Arruns said. "Is it from the shrine of Numa you bring this? Some old artifact of Egeria?"

Instead of answering Arruns, Demetria took the package and turned to Apollodorus. "This is an ancient thing. And we dedicate it now to Apollo," she said.

Apollodorus stood up. "You may part the cloth. I would see this."

Demetria untied the twine. It took some time, because there were several knots. But before too long she was unrolling the cloth and revealing the dull gray horn exterior of the gold-filled *baculum*.

Apollodorus took the staff and ran his hands along it, all the way up to the knob. "There is a hinge," he said.

Lucius came forward and put his hand on the knob. "Secret. Secret. You see?" He pulled back the knob, sighted inside it, then showed it to Apollodorus.

"What is this?" he asked, pointing to the hole in the center. "Is it gold there?"

"Gold inside," said Lucius.

Arruns and Titus sat bewildered. They had, of course, never seen either *baculum*; Arruns had seen Lucius cast something out of a boat through rain and clouds using what might have looked to him like a cornel-wood staff. But no one had ever told them about the two *bacula* of Egeria, the staves of power for the priest-kings of Rome.

And neither of them saw the whites of Lucius' eyes turning gold, for he was careful to keep his back turned to them as he, the simpleton, showed the priest of Apollo the "secret" of the staff.

"Yes," said Apollodorus. He studied Lucius for a long time, saying nothing.

Lucius, instead of looking down as he did most of the time, met the priest's gaze directly.

"What do you wish, father?" Demetria asked.

"You, and you." Apollodorus pointed to Demetria and Lucius. "Come with me. You—" and this was the last thing he said in Latin—"please stay here. We will have the slaves bring you further refreshment. We won't be too long, but if we tarry, feel free to ask a slave to allow you to meditate under the laurel tree. It is a fine spring day and Zeus has given us good weather."

Demetria wrapped the *baculum* again and followed Apollodorus out the door.

Lucius turned to Arruns and Titus. "Cousins," he said. "Good men. Good friends."

::XIV::

Apollodorus said nothing as they left the priests' quarters, walked across the courtyard and through the gate. Still silent, he led them down another staircase, this one at the very edge of the back of the temple. At the bottom of this staircase stood not a door, but a stone slab. The priest touched the slab at a certain place a foot or so above where there might have been a knob on a regular door.

The slab slid, rolled, on a track, out of the way.

"Inside."

The single Greek word made both youths' skin go gooseflesh. This was a holy place—a Greek holy place—and it was as if the word had summoned the god to hover above them.

There was another staircase. It was dark, but in the distance twinkled the light of an oil lamp. This turned out to be on a stand, at the bottom of the stairs. Apollodorus took the lamp from the stand and lit the way forward.

They turned left, went through a stone-lined hallway on which, every few feet, a drip of water came from a crack. More stairs opened into a cavern with a hole in the ground several feet across.

Apollodorus leaned against the cavern wall. The ceiling was too high for the lamp to light.

"Now we wait," he said.

Presently a sound came from the depths of the cavern, a scrabbling, tapping sound. It was not fast or regular but it seemed deliberate. And as the tapping grew louder, Demetria felt more and more unsure. What was coming out of this cavern? Some kind of monster that would take the *baculum* and kill them? It seemed unlikely, and Apollodorus had been friendly. But the echoing sounds were not like anything she had heard before.

Lucius was holding onto his cornel-wood staff, ready to pull off the knob if necessary. He had been in a cavern recently and had been taken by surprise. This time, he would not be.

Presently, however, the tapping sounds became more familiar as the sounds of sandals against stone. For out of the cavern emerged an old woman, dressed in heavy robes, but bareheaded and with her grayish-black hair braided down her back. She was not a monster at all but looked, in a way, like anyone's grandmother.

The youths relaxed.

"Greetings," she said in Latin. "I am the Pythia."

"Greetings, grandmother!" Demetria said, and Lucius hastened to do the same.

"Do not bow or kneel," said the Pythia. "It is not the time for that. Apollodorus, you may go."

"But, my mistress—"

"Apollo knows you are curious. Of course, you are

dedicated to a thorough knowledge of all things, as much as a man might know them. What priest of Apollo would not be? But you must go. This is between these young ones and me. You know why."

"As you wish, my mistress."

When Apollodorus had gone and the echo of his own sandals had died away, the Pythia addressed Lucius. "You are not what you seem, young man. Speak freely, for here all knowledge is uncovered."

Lucius bowed slightly. "I am Lucius Junius Brutus, a prince and master mage of Rome."

She bowed back. "Prince of power from the land of the sunset."

"I..." Lucius paused, not exactly knowing what to do, and feeling a bit shy at the deference shown by the priestess.

Demetria nudged him, and he remembered. "Great priestess, I give this staff as an offering to the god Apollo."

Demetria held it out to the Pythia, and she took it.

"This is the *baculum*. It is one of the great staffs of power of the Roman people, now stripped of its ability by the devices of the Etruscans, but a prized possession and one I pray will be always known as a sign of the friendship between the peoples of Rome and Greece."

In the lamplight, the shaft seemed to shine with an otherworldly glow.

"On behalf of the god, thank you. It is indeed a great gift." She turned it over in her hands, letting the smooth horn of the shaft run against his fingers.

"May I?" Lucius asked.

The priestess gave a slight nod.

Lucius then took the knob, as he had done with Apollodorus, pulling it back using the hinge.

His eyes glowed, as did the gold that filled the hollow shaft.

The priestess gasped as she studied Lucius' eyes. She said nothing for a long instant, then motioned to the both of them. "It is time."

Time for what? Demetria wondered, but kept quiet; a great tightness had seized her throat. She may not have been able to cry out even if a prodigy appeared over Lucius' shoulder.

"Come with me." The Pythia turned and made her way to another stone slab like the one at the entrance of the underground chambers. Another touch, and the slab moved on its track.

Lucius shot Demetria a glance that said, *What's going to happen?*

Demetria shrugged her shoulders and followed the priestess.

The slab revealed stairs descending into darkness, cut from the living rock, and slippery from the beating of many feet upon them.

"This is an ancient place," the priestess informed them. "Here is the resting place of the dragon of Pytho. Do not speak. It is a holy place."

At the bottom of the staircase was another chamber, but this one was illuminated by torches set into holders at the cardinal points of the roughly circular space. On the opposite side of the room from the stairs, the rock jutted out and the torches threw light on a set of petrified bones. The bones seemed to make a long, coiled line, as if they had been of some kind of serpent. At the end of the line a skull, long and narrow, lay embedded in the rock. And in the eyehole of the skull itself sat a gem, gleaming bright green in the torchlight.

"It is the Eye of Pytho. Take the jewel, Greek mageling," said the priestess, motioning to Demetria.

"Me?" The word came out weak and quavery.

"Of course. Reach out. Fear not."

Demetria looked to Lucius, who swallowed hard and nodded.

The bone of the skull that encased the jewel felt brittle, but with sharp edges, almost sharp enough to cut her fingers as she found a way to pry the stone loose. But putting a finger under it made it rise, and so able to be pulled out with thumb and forefinger.

"Oh!" Demetria cried. She'd dropped it and it skittered along the stones of the floor, out of the torchlight.

"Is it slippery, mageling?" the priestess asked with a deep chuckle that sounded like a cough. "Or heavy, perhaps?"

"Is it lost?" Lucius said, in a panicky way that upset Demetria.

Stung and ashamed, she was about to say Of course it isn't you senseless brute, though she was secretly hoping it hadn't fallen down some endless hole into the depths of the earth.

But the Pythia spoke first. "No, Roman. It is at your foot." And she pointed her torch towards him.

Sure enough, it was there, right next to Lucius' right sandal, shining like a star.

"How did you know--?" Demetria whispered.

Lucius bent down and was about to take up the jewel.

The Pythia waved her torch. "Not you, Roman. The Greek. It is hers."

"Hers?" Lucius' disbelief could be heard in his voice.

"Yes. Pick it up, Greek mageling."

Lucius moved away from the jewel while Demetria got down on her hands and knees. This time she swept it with one hand into the palm of the other. It was warm to the touch and indeed just the least bit slippery. It was not big enough to be held comfortably in her palm, like an egg, but it was much bigger than any gem she had ever seen on the jewelry of the women of Greece who lived in Rome. It had multiple flat faces, all the same size, that gave the illusion of its being a sphere.

"You have it," said the Pythia.

"Yes, grandmother," said Demetria. She couldn't believe it. Hers? And the Pythia had called her "mageling." Little mage. Beginner. Was she to be a mage like Lucius? She sneaked a look at him, but his face betrayed no emotion, at least not in the uncertain lamplight.

"Then let us find the great prophecy of Apollo that gives you ownership of this power."

They moved out of this room, backtracking to the corridor they had seen when coming in. Here, after a few paces, could be seen a threshold. Marble pillars about six feet tall and a foot wide flanked it. A strange smell emanated from here, as if something had been burnt and yet still was smoldering. Both Lucius and Demetria had smelled incense before, but this was not as sweet.

"Phew! That's strong!" Lucius said.

"It's not rotten, though," Demetria said, turning to the Pythia.

The Priestess faced them in front of the threshold. "We will not go inside. It is the place where I meet Apollo. Instead, look to the pillars. You can see here written the great prophecy of Apollo."

On the pillars had been scratched numerous Greek inscriptions, all of them from two to four lines long.

The Pythia traced her finger along the left-hand side pillar, making a kind of hissing, warbling whisper that was not exactly Greek but not any other language, either.

"I have found it," she finally said, and motioned for the youths to approach. "It is this one." She pointed.

The words were scratched into the pillar and very small, written in Greek, each letter following the other with hardly a space in between:

When comes the staff of gold from West in Trojan hand,
Thence also comes the priestess who the gods command.

Trojan hand? Command the gods? It made no sense to Demetria yet. "A staff of gold..." she began.

"...in the hand of this one," the priestess finished for her.

"He is... Trojan?"

"The race of Romans comes from Troy."

"It is our legend," said Lucius. "The hero Aeneas was our ancestor."

Demetria remembered. She had not been taught many Roman stories. This one came back to her; perhaps even Lucius himself had told it, but in the depths of the cave it was hard to think of far-off Rome.

"My Greek is not perfect," Lucius was saying. "Does it not mean that the gods shall command the priestess?"

"No," said Demetria quickly. "Then the sentence would say, Thence comes the priestess *whom* the gods shall command. If the gods command, then you must use the striker of that one whom they command. But this 'who' is a namer. One who is doing the commanding."

"Well done," said the Pythia.

"Of course!" Lucius exclaimed. "For in Greek as well as in Latin there is the namer and the striker. But—how can a human command the gods?"

"It is extraordinary," said the Pythia, turning to Demetria. "We have been waiting for you for a long time."

"For me?"

"Yes, child. I must tell you the story first, and then we will speak of power."

::XV::

The Pythia stood in the threshold of the door as she spoke, with the burnt smell still hanging in the air.

"Many generations ago," she began, "came one from the tiny town of Rome who called himself Numé—"

"Numa Pompilius?" Lucius asked.

"Don't interrupt her," Demetria said, annoyed.

Lucius scowled. "I didn't mean—"

"No matter, my daughter," said the Pythia to Demetria, still as calm as before. She pivoted briefly to Lucius. "Yes, young man, that must have been his name, though we know him now only as Numé. He came to us. We were but a small shrine. No great temple here. But the place was ancient and revered by all those round about, and already the bones of the serpent you saw were known and the story of the Far Shooter's slaying of it was well-established.

"This Numé came to us as a student. He wanted to know all about what we did, how we sacrificed, what our holy days were. He said his people needed to learn the ways of the gods and he was their chieftain. He said a goddess had sent him, by the name of, if I remember it, Hegelia."

"Egeria!" Lucius again.

Demetria sighed and rolled her eyes.

But again, the priestess seemed not to be affected by Lucius' outbursts. "We were happy to give him the knowledge he sought. We Greeks are hospitable to guests. After, so it is said, he visited the oracle of Zeus in Dodona and numbers of other places. We asked him, have you no gods in your place, then, that you cannot worship them yourself? And he said, 'My city is now like a sapling that needs care and nurture, but one day it will be such a great tree that it will overshadow all others. It should have a religion that is like the nations it will conquer.'"

The Pythia ran her hand along the pillar, traced the scratchings of Greek letters that spelled out the prophecy about Rome.

"Numé made a great impression on us and we kept his words in mind, for the future is of great concern to Apollo. Indeed, Numé taught us as much as we taught him, for he was wise, and at the end of his stay, when he was to move on to Eleusis and consult the priests of the Great Mother there, we decided to give him a great gift."

Demetria instinctively opened her palm. "This?"

"You gave The Eye of Pytho to Numa?" Lucius said almost as quickly.

"We did indeed. A very great gift, as you will see. But this was the depth of Numé's wisdom: when we presented the jewel to him, he told us to keep it safe and to ask Apollo when it would be proper for Rome to have it. The god replied with the message you see on this pillar."

"And so we put the jewel back in its place and began to wait for the one who would bring the horn filled with gold. We kept the knowledge of Numé alive and passed it down, from old priest to young, confident that, at the proper time, the owner of the jewel would appear. And now, here you are, a Roman who is also Greek."

The Pythia bowed to Demetria, who gave a half-smile and blushed, though not as hotly as she would have if Lucius had not been there. She felt his jealousy and was in the mood to defy it rather than assuage it. She was in Greece; this was her place; if the Pythia of Apollo wanted to give her a gift, so be it.

"And so..." Lucius eyed the jewel, or rather Demetria's hand, which had again closed over it. "How is it that a jewel can command the gods?"

The Pythia said, "It is not the jewel alone that has the power. Long ago, the god Prometheus, who loved humans, came to the great fashioner Hephaestus and asked if there be something that might help us weak humans in this world of suffering and hardship. Hephaestus, out of his compassion for those who suffer (for he himself suffered much pain in his life) created the jewel and persuaded—for the Great Poet reminds us he is also a god of sweet words as well as fine metalcraft—he persuaded the Olympians to grant a favor to the owner of the jewel, as long as the prayer is just. The gods will obey the owner of the jewel who says the proper prayers—and whatever they have the will and power to do, the owner may also do."

"So there is a power of the Greek language as well as the Latin," Lucius said, and at the Pythia's prompting unsheathed his own *baculum* from the wooden staff, and explained its power.

"Yes," said the Pythia after she had understood everything. "But this jewel is different from that which the brother-mage uses. It is not the power of grammar but the power of prayer."

"In Greece, the power to accomplish one's will comes from a proper knowledge of the gods' will. If you ask the proper god or goddess what you want—using this jewel as your passport—they are bound to give it. But if you ask what is not in the power of a god or goddess, then they can no more help you than if you ask a fisherman to make you a pair of shoes, or a cobbler to catch your dinner."

Demetria now said, "And, please, grandmother, can it be anyone who calls upon the gods with this staff? Or does it have to be a Greek?"

"Anyone with Greek blood may call upon the divine ones of Greece. Romans and Etruscans, if they have no Greek ancestry at all, will not be able to use the jewel."

Lucius frowned.

Demetria again: "And can it be anywhere that the gods will answer? Or only in Greece?"

"Anywhere the gods are worshipped, the jewel avails, but the farther from Greece you stray, the less likely the prayer will be effective. Do you know the dwellers of Olympus and what they hold dear?"

"Grandmother, I think so."

"How many are there?"

"I..." Demetria, suddenly shy again, glanced Lucius' way, who shrugged.

"You are the Greek," he said, half-triumphant, half-envious.

"Of course there is Zeus, who is lord of the rain and the

snow and the lightning bolt," Demetria began.

"And other things," said the priestess.

"What other things?"

"Do you not know?"

"Homer says he is father of gods and men," said Lucius.

The priestess turned to him. "Yes, but for what do men pray to him?"

Again, Lucius shrugged.

"And what about Demeter, after whom you are named?"

"Easily!" Demetria said, relieved that she could answer this one. "She makes plants grow. We thank her for a good harvest."

"So when do you pray to her? Before or after you sow the seed?'

"Why, before..."

"And..."

"After, I suppose!"

"And during the growing season as well. If you are to be a priestess, you must understand these things."

"Then is there someone to teach me?" And Demetria looked expectantly at the Pythia, the real question in her eyes rather than on her lips, for she did not want to presume.

"Child, you ask much," she said. "I could teach. But you are not here for long."

"It is a long time, I think," Lucius said. "We arrived just as the answers were being given and now we must wait nearly a month to ask and perhaps more for the answer."

The Pythia could not hide her amusement. "A month! An eternity for a child, a moment for an old lady."

"Is a month long enough to learn of the divine wills of the

Greek gods?"

"It will have to be."

"And so, grandmother, please you, will you teach me?"

"Alas, daughter, I have many duties and the priests guard my time jealously. Even now they must be wondering where I am." She smiled to herself, casting her eyes down. "No, you will have to learn yourself, through as many means as you can. But I will tell you this. Go to the theater. You will find a teacher there. Of that I have no doubt."

"You grant me a great boon, grandmother."

"There is one more thing that I need to know. I think you will use this power for the good of Rome somehow."

"Why, yes, grandmother. It is... we are... under the rule of the Etruscans, but—"

"But?"

"There is a power that is very great among them. The *haruspices.*"

"We know them. They seek to know the future, like we do."

"But there is one among them who wishes to keep power in Rome."

"True enough. Because he knows the future that your Numé first discerned. That Rome will be great someday. And he wants to stop that."

"So..."

Lucius spoke now. "So now, with this jewel, we have the power of two against one."

"Yes, young man. It is clear from what you say that the Etruscan soothsayers have waxed very powerful in Rome—for if they had not, you and your staff would have been able to defeat them before now. No, there is little you can do against these haruspices unless you use both the power of the gods and that of the Latin language. Working together, you will prevail."

"Thank you again, grandmother," Demetria said.

"Before we part, I must tell you one more thing. You must have a good memory concerning this jewel. The power recedes from it with each prayer. You can only ask one favor of each of the immortals. One of Zeus, one of Poseidon, one of Demeter, and so on. At the end, it is worthless, except as a keepsake."

"And how many Olympians will answer my prayers?"

"That, you must learn. For if I tell you, you will forget. But if you seek it out, you will have it in your heart forever."

::XVI::

Titus and Arruns had already begun asking questions before Lucius and Demetria had gotten used to seeing daylight again.

"Tell us everything," Arruns said.

Demetria didn't tell them everything and kept the jewel safe in a fold of her dress.

In the meantime, Apollodorus had told the princes that as a gesture of thanks for the gift of the staff, the Pythia would hear their question among the first in the next set and therefore would be among the first to receive their response.

"Which means that we might be here four weeks instead of six," Arruns said.

"Not much difference, but it is something," Demetria said. She was secretly hoping for more time, to help her find a way to learn everything she could about the Olympians and therefore make the jewel as effective as it could be.

"Someone needs to tell Nauarchus what is to come," said Arruns. "A sailor or two."

"I will go with them," Titus said. "I do not know otherwise what one can do with one's time in this holy town."

Arruns said, "Be careful. We do not want to come home with two princes instead of three."

Titus laughed. "This one—" he pointed at Lucius—"is not a prince. He is a king. Of fools!"

Lucius leaned on his staff. "Prince! Titus. Titus great warrior! Titus great prince."

"Well, maybe he is not as foolish as all that."

Everyone laughed this time.

The afternoon was near spent when they all began the walk back to Tragopagus' house. A few clouds hugged the mountains in the distance, but otherwise the sky was deep blue and as wide and broad as the sea below it.

"This is the gods' country," said Arruns as they walked. "We are almost to Olympus here."

That night, Demetria dreamed that she had climbed all the way to the height of Olympus. But when she got there, she saw only three gods: Zeus, Demeter, and Apollo. "Where are the rest?" Demetria asked in her dream. "That you must seek out," said Apollo. "For if I tell you, you will forget. But if you search for us, you will remember always." Then Zeus spoke a snowstorm into being, which turned into a blizzard and Demetria could see no one.

She awoke with her arms gooseflesh—she had wriggled outside her coverlet, no doubt during the "hike" to Olympus.

The next day, early, Titus packed food and water for the walk down the mountain and assured everyone he would return in three days unless Nauarchus had found a house with good wine and dancing girls. "Better wine than Tragopagus', at least. I have heard the story of Ulysses making the Cyclops drunk on good Greek wine. But I have not tasted any yet."

"We must begin your education," said Lucius to Demetria when they had a quiet moment.

"But with what teacher? The Pythia said we had to inquire at the theater."

"That is our next destination."

Arruns was happy to stay at Tragopagus', for in truth he was a reader of books and liked to spend time alone or with Enetius, dictating. So Demetria told him she would go to Delphi to investigate the place further and take Lucius along with her for company and to make sure he stayed out of trouble.

The two youths dressed in traveling clothes and so did not attract the attention of the two new guards on duty at the gate. There were many vendors and hawkers who wanted them to part with their money, however, and Demetria obliged one of them by buying a small bronze statue of Apollo as a young man.

"He looks like you," she said to Lucius, who managed a smile.

They inquired about the theater with the merchant, who pointed up the stairs that led to the treasuries and the temples. "Keep going past the temple," he said. "It's not much farther than that. When you hear music, you're almost there."

The merchant was right. In the open space in front of the temple a wide path led up again, and before long they did hear music. It was that of a cithara, a stringed instrument that Demetria had always liked.

"All right, boys," came a voice in Greek when the cithara playing stopped. "That's enough. That's more than enough."

The two friends huffed up the hillside a few more paces till they came to a level area. It was not large—perhaps twenty paces wide, sandy, and bordered with a circle of stones. Around this area the hill rose again, somewhat more gently than the mountain behind it, but steeply enough. It was filled with short grass, mostly brown, but with patches of green here and there.

The cithara player was sitting on a stool perched on a flat patch of ground about halfway up the slope, his instrument at his side. Within the circle stood a group of young men, younger than Demetria and Lucius by a few years. There were more than a dozen of them, but fewer than twenty, and they were arranged in loose groups of threes and fours, barefoot and dressed in leggings and short tunics.

"Everyone home for lunch," said the player. He was young, too, with a short beard, narrow face, and alive, bright eyes. He was the type, Demetria thought, who must smile easily, laugh frequently, and not appear to have a care in the world.

But now this bright-eyed young man was frowning, clearly not pleased with the boys standing in the sandy circle below him. "When you come back this afternoon," he said, "I want you all to have thrown the idea of the games out of your mind. Only the dance, by Dionysus, should concern you. Is that understood?"

The boys nodded, some of them said a few words of apology, and then they scattered, presumably home for their daily bread.

When the cithara player caught sight of Demetria and Lucius, the frown left his face. He called to them. "Ho, two worthies no doubt from other lands. Did you happen to see the miserable imitation of a dance that occurred just now?"

"No, I confess we did not," Demetria said. "We just arrived."

"So were you hoping to watch the rehearsal? Are you from another town that has a theater? Or just curious?"

"I am Demetria, daughter of Istocles and Eodice. This is Lucius Junius Brutus. We are from the city of Rome, in the west."

"Looshisjoonius what? What name is that? It is not Greek."

"I am not Greek," Lucius said. "As Demetria told you, we are Roman. My native language is Latin."

"You speak well," said the cithara player. "I was wondering why the fair one was speaking for you. My name is Helioxenus. I am the chorus trainer and director for the theater here at Delphi."

Helioxenus slipped off the platform and walked toward the youths. He bowed and gave them the kind of smile Demetria knew he had in him. "You must come from far off. I thank the gods they gave you safe passage."

"We had hoped to speak to someone from the theater," Demetria said.

"I am he," said Helioxenus. "Let us find a friendly tree. It is not too warm today, but the sun is bright enough."

They sought out the shade of a nearby laurel tree with a stone well next to it. Helioxenus offered them a drink from the ladle that had been left there.

Helioxenus drank, and sighed. "We are rehearsing for a performance that will happen in three weeks' time, when the questions are asked of the Pythia. There will also be a local athletics contest. It is an offering to Apollo, but it will also amuse those who have come and must wait a long time for an answer. I am afraid that this time we must use a local chorus instead of the group that had been promised from the city of Corinth. They have not arrived yet."

"The cities of the Amphictyonic League send dancers as well as soldiers, then?" Lucius asked.

"Yes, they do. Sometimes. Not enough. I must make do with the local boys too often. I think this time we are going to sneak in some girls. Don't tell anyone. But the god, I think, is more angry with bad dancing than he is with a girl in the theater."

"Will you sing, and the chorus dance, then?" Lucius asked. "Where we come from, I have a Greek friend who plays the cithara and the men from the small town near where we live often dance. But they only know one or two dances." He was thinking of the men of Portentia, who danced the story of Cacus and Hercules, while Logophilus played.

Helioxenus smiled again, bright white teeth shining. "Oh, we must have a much bigger repertoire than that. Our audiences come from all over Greece. The reputation of Apollo is at stake. He is a lover of music and where he rules, the music—and the dancing—must be very, very good."

"Apollo is a god of music?" Demetria said. "That is not something I had heard. Where we come from, he is mostly prayed to for the sake of healing."

"Oh, my dear, Apollo has his hand in many things. If he is only a healer in your land, then that must explain why you must come here. For prophecy, I suppose? You have no gods for that in—where did you say?"

"Rome. We do have our ways of knowing what is to come, but... it is a long story why we're here."

"I love to hear stories."

"All that in good time," Demetria said. All of a sudden she was fighting the urge to gaze into Helioxenus' eyes and tell him whatever he wanted to know. "But I must ask. We were sent here by... by the priests of Apollo, who told us that someone in the theater would be able to teach us about the Olympian gods and goddesses. For example, that Apollo is a god of music as well as healing and prophecy."

Helioxenus' stood up straight. "That must have been me they were thinking about. For I have learned much about the gods through the songs I play and dances I direct. Our songs in this theater are almost all about the gods. They are called hymns and recount stories about the gods' great deeds and sometimes how they make us laugh, for they are immortal and often do not trouble themselves with what we consider sad or shameful."

"That is exactly what I need to know," said Demetria. First his looks had charmed her. Now his knowledge was working its wonders. "I—we—would like to hire you as teacher. By the time our question is heard and answer is given, I would like to know as much as possible about the Olympian divinities as you can tell me."

"Why, may I ask?"

Demetria hesitated, looked at Lucius for a moment, and then spoke. "We would like to bring this knowledge back to Rome. We think it might help the people."

Helioxenus laughed. "There must indeed be no gods where you are."

"I know it sounds strange," Lucius said. "But surely if you know so much about the gods, you know that the strangest things happen to mortals and immortals and sometimes we do not know why."

"I thank the gods you speak Greek so well! It is a wonder." Helioxenus bowed to Lucius, still with a little smile making dimples at his cheeks. "And you are correct about mortals and immortals. In my case, I do not know why the Corinthians have not sent their chorus here yet. Though I have, perhaps, a small inkling."

"Oh?" Demetria leaned closer.

"Some of the Corinthians think they should bring their own director instead of letting me decide how the performance should be done."

"You are very young to be a director," Lucius put in.

"But my father Heliologus was director before me here in Delphi," Helioxenus hastened to reply. "And we take our craft very seriously."

"Helioxenus, please," Demetria said. "Will you teach me? We will pay you in good Neapolitan silver."

"I will be very busy from now until the performance," said Helioxenus. "But I have never turned down a good silver coin."

"We will return tomorrow, then? Will you be here?"

"Bring something to eat for lunch. There will be time between our morning and afternoon rehearsals."

"You have done us a great kindness. We will see you then."

And Helioxenus gave them another of those smiles which, Demetria thought, must charm all the girls in Delphi and beyond.

::XVII::

"He is a great talker," said Lucius as they walked down the hill toward the entrance of the shrine. "I didn't know if he would ever ask us about our reasons for coming."

"But what a task he has! To satisfy so great a god as Apollo. And he said he might use girls for this chorus. That is very bold when most of us Greek girls spend our time in the house weaving. Not to say we do not dance at home. We are very graceful, some of us."

Lucius frowned and a bitterness came into his voice. "Let his precious performance be important to him. But what would he say if he knew the problem that is before us?"

"That's something we will not tell him." Demetria raised a finger and spoke deliberately. "Such a talker must have many friends in Delphi. Titus must not find out about you from some town rumor."

"We will make it clear to him tomorrow when we bring money," said Lucius. "Silver is enough to stop the mouths of most."

That evening Lucius found himself missing the company of

Titus—he was loud and spoke mostly of military matters, but he kept up everyone's spirits. Arruns, Demetria, and Lucius by themselves spent dinnertime quietly, and Arruns excused himself early to read one of the scrolls he had brought with him, letting Enetius retire to the slaves' quarters.

Demetria, for her part, was thinking about nothing other than the Olympian gods and goddesses—and perhaps about Helioxenus as well—and so was hardly in the mood for conversation.

Lucius retired early and, with many things on his mind, was up before dawn. He took a walk out to the edge of the hill where one could see Cirrha in the distance. The early morning breeze tugged at his cloak and made his forearm hairs rise with chill. The sun was hidden behind mountains in the east, but the glow of it seemed to make everything just a little sharper for a moment.

The jewel. It seemed to be what Logophilus had meant when he said that the god could give them something to help defeat Lars Nepos. He should have been happy, heartened that now Demetria could stand with him in battle.

But something still tugged at his spirit. Jealousy? Certainly. But what else? He had waited so long for victory, had spent years on the constitution that would give Rome to the Romans. What could be wrong about that? What gnawed at him from the inside? He could not name the feeling—or the spirit that haunted him—and so he turned to go back inside, taking a long last look at the beauty of Apollo's kingdom.

As he turned, he caught sight of Tragopagus. The innkeeper had pulled his cloak over his head so that his face could hardly be seen, but his slew-footed gait along with his rolling belly gave him away. He was walking much faster than was his habit and soon he was gone, bustling along a path down to the central area of the town.

"It is early to be up, even if there is no barley for breakfast," Lucius told himself, but thought nothing further about it.

Demetria woke up impatient to be off to see Helioxenus, but knowing they would have to wait until midday, spent the morning tutoring Arruns in Greek.

"My friends from the far west," said Helioxenus as Demetria and Lucius entered the theater in full sunshine. "Are you ready for school, then?"

"I have many questions," said Demetria. "And we brought you a generous hunk of cheese and bread and olives." These were courtesy of Tragopagus, who had not been present at breakfast. Demetria had requested the food from the cook.

"And I am here because I would be bored witless doing nothing at the inn," Lucius said. He opened a leather bag with the lunch in it.

"It is well that there are two pupils. You can help each other. Let us go to the laurel and the well."

Helioxenus eagerly took the food after they sat down and he ate with such a good appetite that Demetria wondered if he had enough to eat wherever he lived. "First I must ask," she said after he had eaten most of the bread and cheese and was eating olives and spitting the pits in the nearby grass, "What is meant by 'Olympian'? For there are many gods and goddesses throughout the world but only some may be called by this name."

"Yes. And by that it means those who dwell on Mount

Olympus, in the household of Zeus. But it is not so simple as that. For Zeus has his home on Olympus, and his wife and children are there as well, but there are others called Olympians who do not live there, such as Poseidon and Hades, who are Zeus' brothers. Our great poet tells us this clearly."

"So how many gods and goddesses are there in all that are Olympian? I must know for... for the people of Rome."

"Oh, no one knows that, dearest. Some say twelve, others fifteen or sixteen, depending on the stories you have heard and the cities you visit."

Lucius and Demetria gave each other searching looks. They were thinking the same thing: if it was impossible to know exactly who was an Olympian, then who could be asked a prayer? They didn't want to tell Helioxenus about this; they didn't want to say anything about the jewel.

"By Hercules!" Demetria finally said, bewildered.

"Exactly!" Helioxenus said. "Some tales say that he lives in Olympus now; others that he is in the underworld. Such a god is Hercules. Perhaps he goes back and forth to visit as a wife visits her old household on her father's birthday." And he smiled at the thought, as if congratulating himself for it.

"But Zeus certainly is an Olympian," Lucius said. "We can count on that."

Helioxenus looked to the sky and made a sign with his finger like a jagged lightning bolt. "Zeus watches over us and gives the good rain that makes crops grow."

"And sends thunder and punishes evil-doers with his bolt of fire?"

Helioxenus nodded. "And other things."

"What other things?" Demetria this time.

"Zeus protects guests. He is there when a contract is signed and a promise is made."

"But the lightning bolt. That is the most important thing," Lucius said. He was thinking about how they could defeat Lars Nepos. He certainly had made grammars involving lightning, even out of a clear blue sky. And Zeus could send lightning as well. But the question was always the mirror, which, if strong enough, could reflect away the bolt. Or perhaps two bolts at the same time? But did they want to kill Nepos like that? The feeling tugged at him again.

Demetria, for her part, had moved on from Zeus, thinking that contracts and promises might not be of great help in their quest to free Rome. "What about Poseidon? He rules the sea, is it not true?"

"Mariners call upon him to calm the waves when a ship is in danger. But he is also the tamer of horses and the shaking of the earth." And here he took up his cithara and strummed it. "There is a beautiful hymn to Poseidon that I know. I sang it at a festival in a place called Helicon, which is the home of the Muses, not far from here."

Demetria thrilled to hear the music, and was about to ask Helioxenus to sing it, but Lucius broke in with "And when Poseidon is angry, what does he do? What can he make?"

Helioxenus continued to strum absently. "This is a good question, because Poseidon is often angry. He has his trident, a spear with three teeth instead of one. Once he sent a bull to upset the chariot of his own grandson, Hippolytus. And he brought a monster from the sea long ago, when he had built the great walls of Troy for the king there, but the king refused to pay him his wages."

"You know many stories," Demetria said. She sighed. Something about him made her want to sit with him for a long time. She couldn't exactly tell why at the moment—although his handsome face must have been part of the answer.

"Let's continue on," said Lucius. "What is the next one?"

"Which one would you like to hear about?" Helioxenus asked.

"Aphrodite," Demetria said.

Helioxenus smiled brightly. It was a smile that was pleasing Demetria more and more, and Lucius less and less. "She is one of the greatest Olympians, because she is able to make even the great Zeus fall in love. Do you remember that I told you the gods have hymns sung about them? I recently learned one about Aphrodite. It is about how Zeus was jealous of her power and made her fall in love with a mortal man."

"Oh?" Demetria's eyes had gone glassy.

"Yes. His name was Anchises."

"That's a lovely name."

"You think so? It's a story with much sweetness and honey. Everyone loves it when they hear it."

Lucius said out of the corner of his mouth, "If this hymn is supposed to praise the goddess, I don't know how falling in love with a mortal accomplishes that."

Helioxenus stopped playing and was about to answer, but Demetria broke in: "You wouldn't understand, Lucius. You're not Greek, after all."

"I'm not Greek, but I'm not stupid," Lucius shot back.

"By Hercules! You don't need to yell."

"I just want to know—"

"You don't need to know for the good of the Roman

people. Helioxenus has already told us she is able to make people fall in love. That is a great power."

"We should move on," Lucius said.

"I think perhaps Helioxenus needs a rest from teaching." All of a sudden, Demetria felt strongly protective of the poet. These sudden feelings were coming more frequently. "Maybe you'd like to play?" she said quickly. "I would like to hear it."

"I could play something I have created myself." Helioxenus had stayed quiet the whole time Lucius and Demetria argued. Now that he spoke again, his voice was just as sweet, perhaps more so.

"Oh, yes," Demetria said, clapping.

"Is it about the gods? The Olympians?" Lucius asked.

"Well, not exactly. It does have the gods in it. It has Aphrodite, for example."

"Oh, perfect," Demetria gushed.

"By Apollo. I shall give it a try."

Lucius rolled his eyes and twined his arms in front of his chest.

Helioxenus strummed a flourish on his cithara and began:

Aphrodite fell in love with a mortal
But you, love, are not of that kind
I am but a man and one day will die
But your beauty will cause you to live forever.

"It is a wonder!" Demetria cried and clapped again.

"That is not all there is," Helioxenus said.

"I think we have heard quite enough," said Lucius.

"Oh, stop it," Demetria said. "If you don't like it, you can go back to Tragopagus' house."

"I will not leave you alone in the presence of this... mortal man."

"It's perfectly all right."

"No it isn't. I know it wouldn't be perfectly all right with Istocles."

Demetria sighed.

Helioxenus eyed them both before saying, "It is a good start, today. I think you have learned much. I might ask, however, one thing?"

"What is it?" Demetria said. "Anything we can do, will be done."

"Could you tomorrow bring some wine to mix with this good well water?"

"Of course. How silly of us to forget today. We will bring it."

"And one other thing?"

"Yes?"

"The silver."

Lucius paid Helioxenus, who eyed the coin as if he'd never seen anything like it.

The youths kept their peace until they were again outside the walls of the shrine. That was when Lucius said, "I would remind you to keep your mind on the Olympians."

"You're jealous," Demetria shot back. "Just because someone plays a pretty song doesn't mean you have to worry about me like my father."

"Pretty? He was barely in tune."

"Greek music is different from Latin."

"We have very important work, Demetria."

"We have time. Weeks. We do not have to work every moment of every day."

"Well, just hold on to that jewel. Make sure it with you at all times."

"I have it." She did have it, in the fold of her cloak. She wished she might drill a hole in it and run a leather thong through it, so she could wear it around her neck. But yes, she absolutely had it and would not let it go.

In fact...

She thought she might use it before they arrived back in Rome. Certainly not all the prayers would be needed for Lars Nepos, would they? Quite possibly, Aphrodite would not be at all needed.

And she knew about whom she might ask the goddess.

::XVIII::

Titus was not back the next day or the next, so that the company began to wonder what had happened to him. At midday on the third day, Arruns was speaking with Tragopagus about sending a messenger when Titus turned up, leading a white horse.

"He is a wonder, is he not?" said the muscled warrior, patting the flank of the enormous beast. "A lord of Cirrha lent him to me. There will be an athletic competition during the next round of questions and he wants me to compete in wrestling and the horse race."

"How did this all come to pass?" Arruns asked.

"It is a long story, but the short of it is that when you drink wine and meet people in Greece, they invite you to their houses. And this lord is keen on winning the competition over his fellow lords. There is one in particular from Naupactus who is traveling here..."

Titus went on for some time about the local rivalries in the various events that were held in Delphi. Every four years, the great competition called the Pythian Games was held, but they had come in the middle of that cycle. More frequently, local games were held for those who could travel to Delphi in a day or two, in order to worship the god and entertain the seekers of the future.

"Where are Demetria and our Brutus?" Titus finally asked.

Demetria and Lucius were at that moment sitting under the laurel tree next to the well, waiting for Helioxenus. He had not been present the two days before; when he arrived he apologized and said that his "mother" had been ill and was thought to be ready to give up her spirit to the Underworld.

"But, thanks be to Apollo, she is feeling better," Helioxenus explained, cithara in hand. "The silver you gave me paid a healer, who, thank Apollo, was better than the last one I hired." As usual, he went at the lunch they had brought, which included barley bread and salted fish this time.

"Maybe we should begin with Hades, the Lord of the Dead," Lucius said.

Demetria was about to scold Lucius for speaking of the dead just after Helioxenus had given thanks for life, but Helioxenus didn't seem to mind.

"You mean the Rich One?" Helioxenus said brightly. "That is how we speak of him here in Delphi."

"Rich?" Lucius asked.

"Because all good things come from the earth, including gold and silver."

Lucius pursued that line of thinking. "So if you prayed to him to become rich—suddenly to find a great treasure in the ground, for example—that would be something he might grant?"

"I never thought of it that way. I do not think of the Rich

One as giving, but as taking away."

"Taking away the dead to his place," Demetria said swiftly, thinking maybe it would be good to move on.

Helioxenus nodded. "This one is wise already, I think," he said to Lucius, and winked at Demetria.

Demetria felt warm all over. This was turning into a good conversation after all.

Lucius, ever practical, pursued his line of thought. "So let's say you prayed to Hades to take someone away—to kill him. Would he do that?"

"By Apollo, you ask the most curious questions! Do you have an enemy?"

"We all do, I think, but I prefer friends," said Demetria.

"Yes," said Helioxenus. "Yes, I do as well. By far."

Lucius seemed bound and determined not to let the questions turn into Helioxenus and Demetria gazing into each other's eyes, and he hastened to say, "This is only for the knowledge of the people. We need to know what is lawful to ask for."

Helioxenus blinked. "What? Oh, yes. Based on the poets I have heard, I would say that Hades takes only those for whom it is fated to die. Only those, I suppose, whose time it is. Otherwise one might be stepping on the toes of other gods and goddesses."

"Stepping on their toes?" Lucius asked.

"Yes. All gods have their provinces. Places in this world that are their own, where other gods should not trespass. If Poseidon should attempt to play the cithara, perhaps—"

"How absurd!" Demetria said, giving a high-pitched laugh. "Poseidon, play the cithara!"

"Exactly. It would offend Apollo, for music is his to give and take away at his will."

"And I hope very much that you will play for us again today," Demetria said.

"If you like."

"I like very much."

Lucius tried one last time. "And the next god after Hades? Who might that be?"

It was no use. Demetria would hear nothing other than Helioxenus' voice and cithara. She encouraged him to eat his lunch, and after that he played for what seemed to Lucius a very long time on subjects mostly concerning falling in love. Finally, Helioxenus suggested that Lucius and Demetria might join in the chorus he was rehearsing, though to Lucius it was only Demetria that Helioxenus really wanted in the group.

"You said you might have to sneak girls into the chorus," Demetria said. "How is that possible?"

"The costumes and masks hide the dancers' faces and bodies well. It is to be the story of Zeus' overthrow of the Titans and the Giants. We need some more Giants. But mostly, we need folk who are able to dance."

"I would love to do it," Demetria said.

"If it doesn't get you into trouble," Lucius reminded her. "We are here to ask a question of the oracle, not to dance in a chorus."

But Demetria would not be moved.

It wasn't that Demetria was not aware of her task. If anything, passing time with Helioxenus made the task even more urgent. But as she was thinking of Rome and Lars Nepos, she was also thinking about the future of Demetria.

She had been the handmaid of Lucius for some years already and her father had agreed not to marry her to someone while she was doing this service. But she would be twenty soon, and at that age, many Greek girls were considered not fit for marriage anymore.

And what about marriage with Lucius? It was something they had both thought about—for a long time—but at this point they were more like sister and brother than husband and wife. Once Lucius had gotten rid of the Etruscans, he would be expected to lead the city. He would have to interpret and implement the constitution he had written with Logophilus. No doubt he would be arguing about that with his fellow citizens to all hours of the night. His would be a busy, public life, and he would be expected to marry a woman of another important family, not the daughter of a Greek merchant.

And wouldn't life in Delphi be excitement enough for her? Or might she bring this handsome poet and his enchanting cithara to Rome, where they could put on shows for the newly free Roman people? There weren't many poets inspired by the Muses in Rome. Latin was not a language that skipped along like Greek. Neither, for that matter, was Etruscan. Would it not be a beautiful thing to bring Greek poetry to Rome?

All of these questions were turning in to one answer: Helioxenus must marry Demetria.

It was not exactly the only answer, but it was enough to make Demetria run her finger along the smooth facet of the gem she was keeping safe in the fold of her cloak. To make sure that Helioxenus would do all in his power to make her his wife, and to do what she wanted him to do, she would need to spend one of the favors of the Olympian gods.

Aphrodite would need to be asked.

Demetria considered this knowing perfectly well that it would not be possible to ask Aphrodite anything for Lars Nepos if she asked for Helioxenus. But why would they need Lars Nepos to fall in love with someone? Would that make him less dangerous? It was impossible to know. But there were plenty of other gods and goddesses, at least eleven and perhaps more. And Lucius had his *baculum* (not to mention the *ancile*, the enchanted shield of Numa, which could be used as well). It was hardly possible, Demetria reasoned, that they would need this one particular favor.

Yet she hesitated.

"Helioxenus," she finally asked at the end of their time together that day, "surely you have fine sons to whom you are teaching the art of the cithara. You are such a fine teacher, I think."

Helioxenus said, "My dear Demetria, I am not married and will not be, I think."

"But someone is promised to you?"

"Heavens above! We are a poor family. Perhaps some great man will make a donation to the theater and include me in his gift. Then I could choose a wife. But let us speak of other things." He placed a piece of fish on a slab of bread. "I give thanks to the gods for food and wine. I thank Demeter and Dionysus for them, and Poseidon for preserving the men who bring meat from the sea. They keep my soul, spirit, and body together."

Demetria put her hand on Helioxenus'. "We will make a donation to you when we are able. A god will bless us with great wealth. You will see." *Hades will give it*, she thought. He will not be needed to defeat Lars Nepos, certainly not. And then Helioxenus will be rich and Aphrodite will cause him to want to marry her!

Helioxenus looked down at Demetria's hand, then over at Lucius, who was saying nothing. "You Greeks from Rome are curious creatures," he said to her. "I will see you tomorrow, unless my mother falls ill again."

When they parted, Lucius continued on in silence. He did not appear to be angry, but it was clear he was thinking hard about something.

"How many Olympian gods and goddesses do you think there are?" she asked, partly to have something to talk about, partly to reassure herself that using two of the favors would not affect the outcome of their battle.

Lucius welcomed the question, and they pieced together with each other's knowledge the ones that lived on Olympus: Zeus and his wife Hera; their two sons Hephaestus and Ares; Zeus' unmarried sisters Demeter and Hestia; and four of Zeus' other children, Athena, Apollo, Artemis, and Hermes. That made ten. Helioxenus had said that Poseidon and Hades, though not living on Olympus, could be considered Olympian, which made twelve.

Just as they were arriving at Tragopagus' house, Demetria remembered that Helioxenus had mentioned Dionysus, master of wine.

"Thirteen," she said.

"But did all of those agree to grant a favor? I wonder if there is a way to know," Lucius said.

"Perhaps the Pythia does."

"And she told us she would not tell us."

They were not able to finish their conversation. As soon as they entered the front courtyard of Tragopagus, Titus and Arruns popped out of the inn to greet them.

"Inside, quickly," they said. "A message has come from Nauarchus. A strange creature was seen soaring over his boat."

"It is like a bird and yet not a bird."

"It is more like a flying lion. The head of an eagle and body of a great cat with golden wings."

Lucius immediately thought of the lion-sphinxes in the tombs of the Tarquins under the palace. But those had the faces of humans. What they were describing was a griffin. Both were equally Etruscan, however.

"Did it alight somewhere?" Demetria asked.

"No," Arruns said. "According to the messenger, it circled Nauarchus' boat several times, and then flew off."

Flew off where, Lucius wanted to ask. Back to the west, to Rome?

"Have you seen it hereabouts yet?"

"I did," Titus said. "I was out walking and I saw it perched on a tree above Tragopagus' house. It is not a full-sized lion, but big enough, and the wings shine in the sun. I am not a haruspex or an augur, but even I understand that to be a sign that we are being watched—by the same man who pulled a rope through the face of a mirror."

Arruns said, "If it was on an errand from Lars Nepos, it has understood that we are doing what Father has asked of us. Since we lost Uchtave, I have been wondering how they would keep an eye on us."

Later that night, Demetria, Lucius, and Arruns met.

"Titus is right—this monster is a servant of Lars Nepos,"

Arruns said. "I would not be surprised if Nepos intended for all of us to perish on this journey and to make Sextus king when he sees fit."

"That griffin will not be the death of us," said Lucius. "You may count on it."

::XIX::

Lucius slept little that night, waking just after dawn.

He put on his cloak, went outside, and immediately caught sight of the griffin perched in a sturdy branch of the fir tree across a little gully from the house.

"You will not return to your master," Lucius said through gritted teeth. He unsheathed the *baculum* from the cornel-wood and clicked a grammarstone into the chamber. He knew, somewhere inside him, that what he was intending might not end well. But he cast that aside, with only one thing in mind: defeating the griffin and spiting Lars Nepos.

He circled around the tree, then climbed a steep path toward an open field.

The griffin turned to follow his progress, but did not move out of the tree.

"Come on, little one, come to me."

Lucius gained the summit of the path and found himself in tall grass, now perhaps two hundred paces from the tree. Goats were penned not far off. He continued through the field, which was perhaps only fifty paces wide, and clambered around some rocks into an area shaded by low trees.

"Do you know where I am going, lion-bird?"

The griffin spread its wings and flew across the field to another tree. When it alit, it made the tree bow considerably, but it held.

Lucius could just see it through the canopy of the grove he had entered. He made his way through the grove to another set of rocks. He was coming closer to the face of the mountain itself.

Now the path was hardly wide enough for one nanny goat.

Lucius took it, chambering a grammarstone as he did. When he came to the face of the cliff, he turned his back to it, and cast the stone.

"*O sagitta ferrea pecturs leonis*," Lucius said. *I summon an iron arrow against the chest of the lion.*

Lucius smiled grimly. "Let's see how you deal with that."

In mid-air, the stone turned into a shining shaft, cruelly pointed at one end, fletched at the other, to ensure true flight. It flew directly for the griffin. In a heartbeat, it was upon it, piercing it in the breastbone.

And flying through it, and on into the sky, toward the valley and on, if it had the power, to Cirrha.

The griffin did not move.

"A creature of spirit that yet makes a tree limb bow under its weight?" Lucius whispered. "Truly a wonder, Lars Nepos. But try this."

He readied another grammarstone. This time, as he cast, he said, "*Umbra caron facta.*" *May the ghost be made flesh.*

This time the grammar had an effect. The griffin had looked real enough before, but now it seemed to grow larger.

It flapped its wings, gave the cry of an eagle, looked straight into Lucius' eye.

And attacked.

Lucius was ready and fired another iron arrow. It plunged deep into the heart of the griffin—and if this were any other normal beast, it might have killed it. But instead, it faltered, turned end over end in the air, lost several gold and silver feathers, gave a piercing cry, gathered itself, and dived again.

Lucius screamed, "*O scutom fortissimom mani magistri magi*"—*I summon a very strong shield on the hand of the master mage*—just in time for the shield to appear over his left hand and for the griffin's beak, which was poised to snap Lucius' neck in half, to crunch noisily against it.

The backdraft from the griffin's wings, however, buffeted Lucius and put him off balance, unaccustomed as he was to the weight of his super-strong shield. He stumbled, but righted himself on the stone face of the cliff, even as the griffin reached around the shield with a claw and raked the other side, making contact with his unprotected arm.

The strike did more than sting. It drew blood in a long red stripe, slicing the sleeve of Lucius' tunic clean off. The youth almost dropped the shield because of the pain.

With a Herculean effort he raised the shield and began another grammar. "*O leon volans*—*" He was intending to summon another griffin that would fight the first, knowing that a blade alone might not be enough.

But he couldn't get the words out before the griffin used its wings to leap into the air with an eagle-like *scree!* and over the top of the shield.

Lucius dropped the *baculum* and used both hands to bring

the shield over his head, which again stopped the beak but didn't stop the monster from bashing him to the ground.

The shield, now wedged diagonally against the cliff and a sharp rock next to the goat path, covered Lucius for the moment and in fact saved him: it was not just a flat piece of metal but like a dome, so that the edges themselves made a kind of roof that Lucius was able to shelter under and not be crushed.

As the griffin's claws searched around the shield again, he tried another grammar. "*Scutom leonem adurens.*" *May the shield be burning the griffin.*

It was a good choice. It meant that the front of the shield became super-hot while the back remained cool, because he had not intended for the shield to burn him.

The griffin screamed and withdrew, just long enough for Lucius to roll away from the shield and summon another arrow, this time locating it in the griffin's eye.

O sagitta oculum leonis.

The arrow plunged into the head of the griffin and it reared up, beat its wings so fiercely that it brought up a cloud of dust and straw, blinding Lucius for a moment.

When the dust cleared, the griffin lay on the ground, dead.

Lucius' lungs heaved for air. His arm felt as if a hot iron rod had been laid against it. His ears rang from the blows of the monster on the shield. His first thought: *I might better have left that thing spirit.* But he was happy to have defeated it.

When he had recovered his breath, he looked up.

Something was glowing in the tree opposite the meadow, and it wasn't the sun, for that had risen above the mountains and was giving its general light to the whole world.

No. It was another griffin.

It spoke.

"Are you a simpleton, then? I thought not."

And laughed.

It was the voice of Lars Nepos.

"*Scutom Nepotem haruspicem*," Lucius muttered, casting a grammarstone at the shield. *May the shield attack Nepos the soothsayer.*

It flew into the air and disappeared, on its way, no doubt, to Rome.

"May it hit you over the head and make you into a fool," Lucius said. But he said no more. He went down on one knee, holding his arm where the griffin had slashed it.

When he had healed it with a grammarstone, he was able to get up and walk back toward town, wondering all the time what he could say to Demetria.

"Certainly you should have left it spirit," she said when she heard the story. "How many grammarstones do you have left?"

"A good number. Perhaps two dozen."

"You used many on this fool's errand."

Lucius hung his head. Nothing was going right for him, but all seemed to be more than well for Demetria.

"Why didn't you speak to me?" Demetria asked. "Normally we do everything together."

"You've been doing so well on your own with this jewel and Helioxenus." Lucius scuffed the ground with a sandal. "You might as well go up against Lars Nepos by yourself."

"Don't talk like that!" She paused for a moment, as if gathering her thoughts, then spoke measuredly. "Helioxenus means nothing to me. Our task before us—that's what I'm thinking about."

"Except for the singing and dancing."

Demetria bit her lip. "All right, all right. But how can you blame me? It's not as if we were betrothed."

"You and Helioxenus?"

"No, you simpleton. You and I."

Now it was Lucius' turn to take a moment to think. They both thought often of this, but spoke of it seldom, and so it was difficult to put his thoughts into words. Finally he said, "I do not know... if it would be a good match..."

"Because you are a prince and I am the daughter of a merchant."

"Yes, and..."

"And what?"

"And perhaps Istocles would prefer for you to marry a Greek."

"And what about you, Lucius Junius Brutus? Who would you prefer to marry? A Roman?"

"My father..."

"I didn't say your father. I said you."

Clearly Lucius took too long to open his mouth for the purpose of answering that question, because Demetria shook her head and left before he was able to.

The next day Demetria flirted less with Helioxenus and they spoke of Artemis, Lady of the Wild and mistress of animals, Demeter, who ruled the harvest of grain, and Hestia, also Zeus' sister, who lived in the hearth-fire of every Greek household.

"Fire," Lucius said. "I suppose you could ask this goddess to bring fire to you."

Helioxenus raised his eyebrows. "She protects the family."

"Protects," said Demetria, thinking hard.

"She shall be your last resort," said Lucius.

Helioxenus moved on, though it was clear he was curious what Lucius meant by "last resort." "If you would like a hot fire, you might ask Hephaestus, for he creates things out of fire. Metal things."

"Exactly. Ask Hephaestus to create a spear, a shield, or a sword."

"Achilles, the great hero, asked his mother Thetis to ask Hephaestus to make for Achilles a great shield. It was so curiously wrought, it took the poet Homer many lines of poetry to describe it, and it took me many hours to memorize those lines."

This caused Helioxenus to launch into a recitation of the scenes and characters on Achilles' shield, and this was so fascinating that both youths found themselves caught up in the description, until, after a few dozen lines one of the boys from the chorus arrived and Helioxenus ended the lesson in favor of rehearsal.

"And what about the girls?" Demetria asked. "The ones you're going to add."

"We rehearse at Philocasta's house, in the evenings. You should come. Very secret, however."

"I will. If you tell me where Philocasta's house is."

Helioxenus proceeded to go into a long description, which Demetria appeared to follow.

Lucius was relieved. The less time Demetria spent time with him, the less he would have to answer questions about marriage. Of course he loved Demetria, but he knew that if he were to be an important man in the new constitution of Rome, he would not be as respected or have as many friends among the good families of Rome if he married Demetria. She was right: to marry the daughter of a Greek merchant was not appropriate for a prince of Rome.

Meanwhile, the griffin continued to appear in the fir tree across the gully from Tragopagus' house, almost never moving, just watching.

"I am off to Philocasta's," Demetria said after dinner that night. "It is not far, but I will probably not be home before you are in bed."

"Say hello to Helioxenus for me," Lucius said.

Several hours later a knock came on Lucius' door. He asked who it was, and opened for Demetria. She came in, carrying a lit lamp, and her face was pale in its uncertain light.

"What is it?" Lucius asked.

"I can't believe it," she said.

"Can't believe what?"

"The jewel. I lost it."

::XX::

Demetria had brought the jewel with her to Philocasta's. Why not? Shouldn't keeping it safe mean having it with her at all times?

When she had arrived at the house, a dozen girls greeted her warmly in the hearth room, all several years younger than she and full of chatter, questions, and news.

"How did you meet Helioxenus?" one asked.

"Are you really from the far west?" asked another.

"Helioxenus must wish you truly for his bride!" said still another, and they all agreed. "You are as beautiful as a goddess!"

The first rejoined, "And look at her strong arms. You have already woven much wool in your day. Whoever marries you will become rich just from your work!"

They said a good many things of the same nature, and Demetria thought this all very silly, but just the same it felt good to be admired. There was something comfortable about being in the women's quarters, she had to admit. Though she was always trying to escape them as a girl, she always came back to them.

Home.

The girls took her to the second floor of the house, reached by a narrow set of stairs. There, many looms were set up, along with beds, tables and chairs, and trunks for clothing. A finished rug with the face of Apollo woven into it was hung on one wall.

"Do you all live here?" Demetria asked.

Not all did, she discovered. Some had sneaked out of their houses as Demetria had done when she was their age, but all were related somehow, cousins of the three daughters of Philocasta. A few were cousins of Helioxenus himself.

"But where is the man?" Demetria asked. "Are we not to dance for him today?"

An older woman had entered the women's quarters behind Demetria, and now spoke. "All in good time. I am Philocasta. You must be Demetria."

"Yes, mother."

Philocasta may have seen forty summers; she had gentle wrinkles about her mouth and eyes, which were warm and full of spirit. She had let her long, graying hair down but had not braided it yet for the night.

"Sit and refresh yourself first," she said. "We are pleased you wish to serve Apollo in the dance. We here are all proud of Delphi and our god and our performances in the theater must be of the highest quality. Where you come from, do the women dance in public?"

"No, mother. I may say that in Rome, the Greeks are more Greek than the Greeks in Greece."

Everyone thought this was the cleverest thing anyone had

ever said, and they laughed and applauded.

It struck Demetria then this must be a good place to have one's home.

A girl gave Demetria a cup of wine and a cake sweetened with honey and studded with pine nuts and fresh rosemary. It was still slightly warm and moist, smelling of the herbs and honey.

"You must understand, Demetria," Philocasta said, "that we Delphians do spend most of our time at the loom, as the fathers ask. But when it is a matter of pleasing the god, we do our duty willingly."

Demetria bit into the cake. It tasted as good as it smelled. "And will no one know that you are women doing these dances?"

"No, indeed," said Philocasta. "And no one must speak of it. It is a great shame for women to be seen in the theater, but it is a greater shame for the boys to spoil the performance."

"Is there no one who can dance among the boys, then?"

"There used to be, but they have grown older and must take on other duties. The young ones we have now are just learning. But we women do our dances among ourselves and all of us know very well to learn new ones."

Just then a knock was heard on one of the shuttered windows.

"It is Helioxenus!" several of the girls cried, but Philocasta shushed them.

"We must now go down to the courtyard to rehearse," said Philocasta. "My husband has gone to our ancestors, and my son, who keeps this household now, stays out late at night to drink wine with his friends and talk about the harvest. Let us make haste and do all we can in the time we have."

Helioxenus, it turned out, had climbed the wall of the courtyard, walked along it putting foot over foot till he came to the house itself. He was tall enough to reach up to the second floor and knock on the shutters. Then he shimmied down from the wall on the thick vines that covered it.

Armed with his cithara, the director quickly explained the dance and arranged the girls. It was to be a tale of the battle of Pytho, the great serpent, against Apollo. This dance would concern Apollo's role in the battle as archer. The girls' roles would be to create a serpent by creating a snaky, sinuous line, with a lead girl wearing the mask of Pytho herself.

But it was not so simple as all that, as Demetria soon discovered. There were intricate gestures to be learned, and swirling movements back and forth. And there must be patience as well, for the dancer who played Apollo would have his own time to shine, his own dance.

"Who will be Apollo, then?" Demetria asked.

"You, dearest," said Helioxenus, and everyone gasped.

"You are a head taller than all the rest of these," he continued. "And we can give you boots that make you even taller. You are older and, may I say, stronger than the girls."

Demetria looked over the group, many of whom might not yet have been able to bear children. They were skinny and all knees and elbows, whereas she had put on weight as she grew older. "It is well that you say stronger, and not another type of word," Demetria said.

Philocasta laughed. "Wait until you become a mother, my dear. You will be very strong, then."

It was a wonderful night. Demetria loved the idea of being

the one everyone counted on, and though she had never danced in public before, the idea of having a costume and mask made it easier to think that it would be possible. Helioxenus supported her, as did Philocasta, and all the girls adored her. What could be better?

At the end of the night, Helioxenus caught her by herself and took her hand. "You have done so well tonight," he said. "It is as if you have been dancing all your life."

"You are such a great help," Demetria managed. His grip was strong yet gentle, and it made her melt with desire. *Surely this is my husband*, she thought.

"I make bold to do this, but you are so beautiful," he said, and kissed her softly on the cheek.

"Helioxenus," she whispered.

"I will see you tomorrow and tomorrow and tomorrow. Please the gods."

"Please the gods."

On the way home, carrying a lamp provided by Philocasta, she was full of thoughts of the future. There was so much to arrange! She would need first to help Lucius with the Etruscans. Then she would be free to return to Delphi. So first she would need to make sure the jewel was safe.

She fished in the fold of her cloak, just to feel the jewel. She knew it had to be there. She wouldn't have dropped it. That would have been foolish and she was not in the least a foolish person.

But her hand did not light or land on the smooth surface of the gift. Instead, Demetria felt linen, nothing but linen, the fabric of her cloak. She tried again, putting down the lamp in the street, and finally taking off the cloak itself and shaking it.

The jewel was not there.

"How could you have done such a thing?" Lucius asked irritably.

Demetria felt as if she had fallen from a great mountain. One moment she was in the heights, breathing in the pure air of heaven, and the next she was far below, looking up at Lucius' alarmed face.

"I don't know. I was doing a lot of dancing, a lot of bending over. It might have fallen out while we rehearsed."

"But you would have found it on the ground then, would you not?"

"Perhaps. Someone could have kicked it to the side or under a table. There were torches, but it was not lit as if by the noonday sun."

"That's just it, though. In the torchlight, the jewel would have sparkled and be seen."

Demetria repeated "perhaps," thinking it a silly thing to say, but nothing else came to mind.

"And what if your lover Helioxenus took it?"

"Nonsense! Of course he didn't take it! He is—he's—" Demetria found herself considering the possibility. He had been the only one close enough to have taken it, when he leaned in and kissed her. But that was absurd. She would have felt his hand in her cloak.

Unless...

"There's only one thing to be done," said Lucius. "I must make a grammar to retrieve the jewel."

Demetria would normally have said that that was a good idea, perhaps the best one in the circumstances. But now she hesitated. She didn't want Lucius to know—indeed, she didn't herself want to know—whether Helioxenus had somehow been a cause of the jewel's disappearance.

"I can find it. I can go back to Philocasta's courtyard. It has to be there. Don't waste a grammarstone."

But Lucius had already brought a stone from the pouch at his side and was weighing in his mind the words he would use to retrieve the jewel.

"Lucius, don't," Demetria pleaded.

"*Gemma Delphica deorum et deasom Graecorum precibos motorum mani magistri magi,*" Lucius said. *May the jewel from Delphi of the Greek gods and goddesses moved by prayers be in the hand of the master mage.* He had been very specific about the jewel. Who knows how many jewels there were in the world associated with the Greek gods and goddesses?

"It will fly to us," said Lucius, after casting a grammarstone into the night. "And that will be the end of that."

Demetria thought of the jewel in some box in Helioxenus' house, rattling about, and then Helioxenus undoing the latch and watching in wonder as the jewel rose in the air to find a way out. Would he say anything to her about it? Or was she worried for no reason? Was the jewel in some corner of Philocasta's courtyard, kicked there by a dancer, maybe even herself?

She might never know.

Time passed. Lucius kept open the shutters of his room and looked out into the darkness. From time to time he held out his palm to the sky, making a fist, then extending his fingers, to give the jewel a target to find.

"Why is it not here yet?" Demetria asked finally, after perhaps a quarter of an hour. They had been silent all that time, both, no doubt, with the same question on their minds.

"The grammar should be perfect. It was accurate."

"Yes, it was. No errors made."

"Perhaps the jewel was destroyed."

"Don't say that. If it is of the gods, it can't be destroyed."

"But shattered, perhaps?"

"Who would do such a thing? And how?"

"I don't know. Nepos?"

The name chilled them, and neither spoke it again, until the evening breeze, cool as it was, made the hairs on their arms stand up.

Lucius closed the shutters. The sound of it was like the shutting of a door to a prison.

"I'm sorry," Demetria finally said.

Lucius sighed. "The gem may not be so close by," he said. "I don't know if the grammarstone found its target." He rubbed his eyes. "But I am tired now. We should sleep. Whoever has it—" he didn't says Helioxenus, for he knew it would sting Demetria—"cannot understand its power. They must think it only something to be cherished or sold away for much gold. I will consider this and so should you."

Demetria threw her arms around Lucius' neck. "Don't be angry at me. We'll find it."

"I'm not angry," Lucius said, and for the first time his voice lightened. "I was jealous of this jewel. You were right. If we never find it, then it is up to me to defeat Lars Nepos and free Rome. Which is what I wanted all along."

Demetria wiped away a tear. "It is not up to you. We'll do it together, as we always do."

Lucius turned to her. "I will need you, *arana*." Their own

word for friend.

"I will be there, *arana*."

::XXI::

While she lay in bed, Demetria thought of a conversation they had had with Helioxenus about Hermes, in between songs and gazing into his eyes, and it somehow made more sense now.

"And what about Hermes, the messenger of Zeus?" Demetria had asked.

"Why, he is the cleverest of all the gods," Helioxenus said. "I would say that after Dionysus, he is the Olympian I pray to the most."

"He is more than just a messenger, taking a word from Zeus to those of us below?" Lucius asked.

"Much more. He is always thinking of what might benefit him and those who protects. He is a thief. He stole Apollo's cattle, you know."

"I heard that," Demetria said. Her aunt Phane had once told her this story.

"But you see, he also created the lyre out of a tortoise shell, and he gave it to Apollo as a gift. Which is why our god is so concerned with music. And anyone who is interested in speaking and lying and getting what he wants should pray to Hermes. If you are a merchant, pray to Hermes to make others wish to buy your wares. If you are a diplomat, Hermes will make you clever to have kings agree to what your king wants them to do. All travelers pray to Hermes for a safe journey as well. He is a wayfarer himself, you know."

Lucius nodded. "But for journeys at sea, he is not so important," I think.

"No, Poseidon is the one who is moved by prayers for that. But it would not hurt to pray to Hermes for a safe sea journey. And also the divine twins, Castor and Pollux. They have charge over ships to save them from storms."

"But these are not Olympians."

"Perhaps not. It depends on the story, of course."

Demetria fell asleep without admitting to herself what this must mean, but she woke the next morning with the inescapable conclusion that Helioxenus must be a thief, just like Hermes.

After breakfast, Lucius and Demetria raced to the theater, only to see quite a different sight from what they had been expecting.

Two dozen young men dressed in identical white linen shirts and leggings were ranged around the dancing floor. Some were talking, others stretching their legs. Helioxenus was nowhere to be found.

"Are you the director?" One of the men asked Lucius when they approached.

"Who are you?" asked Demetria.

"We are the chorus from Corinth," said the man. "We just arrived last night. What a wretched journey! All uphill beside a cliff! Do you know where the director is?"

At once, Demetria's face fell. She would not play Apollo, nor would any of the girls dance in their own town's theater. The Amphictyonic League had sent the contingent they had promised—just a little later than Helioxenus or anyone in Delphi expected.

They hurried to the temple of Apollo, where a priest was attending those who had come to register their questions that day. He told them where Helioxenus lived, and they set off to that place.

Neighbors helped along the way. The house was down the hill, among olive groves. A stone wall terraced a small plot of land where vegetables grew. A communal well stood nearby. The house itself was made mostly of the same stone that terraced the ridge. It was small, without even a door; just a curtain of heavy linen hung over the threshold.

Lucius was the first to enter, pushing back the curtain and calling for Helioxenus. It was dim inside—no lamps burned, and light came through a single, small window that was a place where stones had not been laid in the wall.

An old woman sat on a low bench next to a hearth fire that was mostly embers. She was tending a small pot of peas in the ashes at the edge of the fire. The smell of it told them she had skill with herbs and salt. She had on a cowl over her robe; though they could not see her face, both Lucius and Demetria could tell by her hesitant movements that she was very old.

"Grace be to you, mother," Demetria said.

The woman looked up, but said nothing.

"We seek Helioxenus. Is that your son?" Lucius asked.

She continued to stare.

"Do you know where he is?" Demetria asked.

She shook her head and tapped her ears, then shook her head again.

"I think she is deaf," Demetria said.

Lucius clapped his hands sharply twice.

Little reaction came from the woman, except a slight narrowing of her eyes and a stare that meant them no good.

Lucius then took out a grammarstone, leaned over the woman, and placed it in her ear. *"Femina iuveniis audiens et loquens,"* he said. *May the woman be hearing the youths and speaking.*

The woman put her hand to her ear and clutched Lucius' hand.

The grammarstone had disappeared.

She looked up at him with wild eyes.

"Can you hear, mother?" Demetria asked. "Can you hear me?"

Slowly, the woman nodded her head. "Great Apollo," she whispered over cracked lips.

"Can you tell us where your son is? Can you tell us where is Helioxenus?"

"The gods! Are you gods?"

"No," said Lucius. "But Helioxenus has something that is ours. It is of the gods."

He is not my son, nor my grandson," she rasped, and nodded. "But he is a good boy."

"We need to find him."

"He has gone away," she said after a time. She put her hand out and tapped it three times. "He said he would be gone three days. It was our way of speaking."

"But if he is gone, who will look after you?"

"I can look after myself."

"Did he show you something? Something precious?"

"A green gem."

"Yes, that was it. What we stole from us!"

"I told him it was bad luck. But he wanted to make a better life for me. He went away to sell it."

"Where? Where did he go?"

"Perhaps to the town below. Perhaps to Athens. Do you own it?"

"It was a gift," said Lucius. "It was from the Pythia."

The old woman nodded again. "I knew it was bad luck the moment I saw it."

Demetria said, "It is not bad luck to us. It is something we must have."

"May the gods return it to you, children. Helioxenus is a good boy. He would not take something not his own unless he had great need."

When they left the house and emerged again into the sunshine, Lucius hit his fist into his open palm. "No idea where he went? Or maybe she does, and is just trying to protect him. He's a good boy, after all!"

"I don't think so," said Demetria. "But he could have gone anywhere. We'll need to use a grammarstone now to find him."

"Make him fly here?"

"Dangerous, if he's inside! I wouldn't want to try to pull him out of a locked house."

"Or we could ask for the way to be shown to us and fly there."

"Tonight, after everyone is in bed and no one sees us."

"Agreed."

Iuvenees volantees homini gemmam Apollonis portanti was the grammar they chose: *may the youths fly to the person carrying the jewel of Apollo.*

But again, nothing happened. They were not borne into the air at all.

"How is this possible?"

"Maybe he's not carrying the jewel."

"But we said 'person.' If he's sold it, it should take us to whoever has it now."

"We have to think of a better grammar. What's the use of a grammarstone if it doesn't work?"

"I wish we had the jewel! What god do you ask to find lost things?"

"Lost?" Lucius blinked. "Not lost. Stolen." And he took out another grammarstone. "*Iuvenees volantees ventod furi gemmais Apollonis.*" *May the Roman youths fly by the wind to the thief of the jewel of Apollo.*

Immediately they were borne into the air, a powerful gust whipping their cloaks and casting dust into their eyes. They joined hands as the wind took them higher and the evening chill stiffened their cheeks and made their eyes water.

"It must be a short flight," Demetria said into Lucius' ear. "He can't have gone a long way."

And so it was. They did not know where they were going in the dark; there were few lights on the ground to guide them, and Lucius didn't want to create a light with a grammarstone and thereby disclose to anyone happening to look up that two youths were flying unaided over their heads. However, it took very little time for the grammar to do its job. They alit very quickly and found themselves in a damp field of grass behind

Helioxenus' own house. A tumbledown stone shed revealed itself when Lucius did make a grammar light. They had come down right next to its entrance.

"Could he have been so close all this time?" Lucius whispered. "And his mother protecting him?"

Demetria said nothing, but approached the shed, which like the house had no door. At one time it may have kept a goat or two from getting wet during a rainstorm, but now its roof held only a few sticks and no tiles.

In the dim light of the grammar, Helioxenus could be seen sprawled on a bed of dry grass, his cloak pulled close at his neck.

"Helioxenus!" Demetria called. Was this the same man who had been so convincing as the leader of a secret dance troupe, the one who had all but asked for her hand in marriage?

In response, a snore.

"Helioxenus! Wake up!" Lucius knelt next to him and shook him by the shoulder.

"Dark still," came Helioxenus' response. "Leave in the morning."

"No, you're not leaving in the morning. You're staying right here."

At this, the chorus master opened his eyes, just for a moment. Then he screwed them shut. "Light! Too bright!"

"It's Demetria, Helioxenus. We need to find the jewel you stole from me. It wasn't yours and it's important to us."

Helioxenus groaned. "Cursed. Don't have it anymore."

"We know you don't have it," Lucius said. "We need to know where it is."

Finally, Helioxenus sat up, rubbing his eyes. "I just did get to sleep. It's difficult out here, you know. Scratchy hay, beetles crawling over me. Do you have any food to share?"

Demetria felt irritated and betrayed, but Helioxenus was so wretched, she could almost pity him. "Why don't you just go home?" she suggested, fighting to keep her patience. "Did you know that we were there this afternoon, looking for you?"

"No. Hid in a cave today during daylight. But at night, the bats come out. *Brrrr.* I've never liked them."

"We're wasting time," Lucius said. "Tell us where the jewel is. Did you sell it to someone?"

"No." The chorus master's tone was sharp and definite. "I knew the jewel was unlucky almost as soon as I... took it."

Demetria's eyes narrowed. "Did you learn so well from Hermes your trade? Did you take it when you kissed me?"

"Kissed you?" Lucius drew back.

Helioxenus winced. "I'm sorry for that. But you have to understand. We are poor. If you met my mother—who is not my mother or grandmother but a distant cousin of my father—you'd know that we live on very little."

"Do you not get pay for your work with the chorus?" Lucius asked. "And what about the silver we've been handing you for your lessons?"

"I do receive a little pay, but almost all of it is taken in repayment of a debt my father incurred long ago. A merchant in Cirrha convinced him to buy a shipment of perfume and sell it abroad. He hadn't enough money to buy it, so he borrowed from a moneylender. The ship went down to the bottom of the sea with the perfume. Ever afterwards, we were in debt rather than rich."

"A chorus master had better stick to what he does best,"

Demetria said.

"And the jewel?" Lucius' tone was stern. It was clear he wasn't feeling sympathy for the unfortunate Helioxenus.

"I didn't take it on my own. The innkeeper—what was his name—told me he would pay very much for it if I could bring it to him."

"Tragopagus?"

Helioxenus snapped his fingers and pointed at Lucius. "That's the one. He told me he could get me a tenth of a talent of silver, which is enough to pay off the debt and a bit more."

"A lot of money for an innkeeper to have."

"I didn't question how he could get it. I was just thinking of the debt. So I deceived you, Demetria. I am quite sorry for it. But I still want you to play Apollo. That wasn't a lie."

"The troupe from Corinth has arrived," Demetria said. "There's no need for me anymore."

Helioxenus gave a slow nod. "I thought perhaps they might come. But in the theater, there must always be... a second way."

"You still haven't said what you did with the jewel. Is it with the innkeeper?" Lucius pressed.

Helioxenus said, "No. I was thinking about it, but almost as soon as I... came into possession of it, I noticed a strange bird—well, a strange creature—was following me as I made my way home."

"Creature?"

"It was hard to see, but when I had my hand on the jewel I could see it better. It glowed in a way. It had the body of a lion—its tail and four feet and claws—but the wings and head of a bird."

"A griffin. Lars Nepos' griffin."

Helioxenus went on, as if he hadn't heard Lucius. "I had almost made it home. It followed me, never closely but always there. Then the jewel flew out of my hand as if a god had taken it—"

"Flew out of your hand?" Lucius cut in.

"Yes, and it was gone, like that. But then the griffin must have caught it in its teeth—"

"Caught it in its teeth?" Now it was Demetria's turn to interrupt.

"Yes, and it swooped down and deposited the jewel back in my hand."

"So that's why the grammar didn't work!" Lucius cried.

"I went to my grandmother and told her I was going away," Helioxenus said, "but I only meant to hide. Without seeing the innkeeper, I hurried to the spring of Castalia and threw it in as an offering to the god. The... griffin... is that what you called it? It flew away as soon as I did the deed and I haven't seen it since. Surely bad luck cannot follow someone who gives something valuable to Apollo?"

Demetria snapped her fingers. "The spring of Castalia! But if it is in a pool, it should have flown out of the water when we named it."

"I don't know what you mean by 'named it,'" Helioxenus said, "but the spring of Castalia has many twists and turns in its depths," said Helioxenus. "When something falls in it is not able to be fished out again."

"That is impossible. It must be able to come out."

"We will need to visit it in the morning," Demetria said. "In the meantime, go back to your mother, Helioxenus. She is no

165

doubt lonely and needs you."

"But I told her I would come back with money."

"You are like your father," said Lucius. "You do not think carefully about the deals you make before you make them."

The snap of a branch behind them made both youths startle.

Lucius whirled around, readying a grammarstone.

::XXII::

"Never fear." A raspy, weary voice.

Helioxenus gasped. "Mother! You speak!"

"And hear," she said. "Thanks to these two." She joined them and put her hand on Demetria's shoulder, leaning slightly against her. "I could not sleep tonight, waiting for you. I heard them arrive and then you began to speak. It is not honorable what you did, for these are friends, but I know you wanted to help."

Helioxenus nodded. "Forgive me, mother."

"Strangers, I might be able to help, a favor for a favor. My son has said he threw this jewel into the holy spring. I know something about this spring, for I am kin to the Pythia who gave you this jewel. Once long ago there were three of us sisters who might have been the Pythia—and I was the eldest by far. But the lot fell to the middle, the one who is the Pythia now, and I became the wife of a priest."

She sighed, as if remembering days long past, both good and ill. "Our family used to tell a story about the spring, that there is a cavern far below here, on the valley floor, where the water of the spring comes out after cascading down within the mountain. You may be able to enter there and seek after the jewel through the caverns. For most it would be a fruitless quest, but if you can make the deaf to hear and the mute to speak, then maybe this would be child's play to you."

"Not so easy as that," Lucius said, "but we have been in caverns before, Demetria and I."

"It is well. But beware, for the cavern is guarded. Apollo rules Delphi, but there are more powers under the earth than the Olympians."

"But we are not coming to plunder, only to take what is ours," Demetria said.

At this the old woman shrugged, but said nothing.

Demetria and Lucius turned to each other but they, too, said nothing. There was no need.

Lucius said, "Is this all the advice you give, mother?"

"How precious is the treasure to you?" she rasped. "More precious than your lives?"

Lucius said, "I need this to save my city. I would stake more than my life on it."

Demetria swallowed, but said, "And I."

"Then go. You have power to make light and there are still many hours before Dawn's horses chase away the darkness."

"Thank you, mother," Demetria said, taking her hand and Lucius hastened to add his thanks.

"It is not you who should thank me. Rather, respect the gods, that they might give you what you wish. Now, Helioxenus, come inside. There is still some pea stew for you to eat."

"Thank Apollo and all the gods!" Helioxenus exclaimed.

"My pride might have made me starve to death!"

With a grammar, the youths were easily able to find the entrance to the spring of which Helioxenus' mother spoke. It was hidden, nevertheless, in a thickly wooded gulley at the bottom of the mountain, impossible to see from the banks of the river wending through the valley. Wild olive trees, pine, and fragrant laurel overhung a rocky stream that gurgled noisily into the main river. It would make for a shady place to bathe in the heat of the summer, with water that was cold and clear. Now, it was impossible to do otherwise than wade through it with heads bowed, pushing branches out of the way.

Demetria cried out in frustration more than once as her hair was caught on low-hanging twigs.

Lucius, for his part, managed to turn his ankle on a shifting stone in the water. But after perhaps a quarter-hour of hard going in the dim light of a grammar, they found themselves at the entrance of a cavern, portal-like in shape, half-again as tall as they were, and quite wide, at least wide enough for three to walk abreast.

"Look!" Demetria pointed to the top of the opening. Greek letters had been carved into it.

"What does it say?" asked Lucius. "I can't quite make it out."

"*Gnothi seauton. Know thyself.*"

"That's strange. Is it advice? Know thyself." Lucius sat down on a rock and took off his sandals, massaging the ankle he'd hurt. "I'd say I do know myself. I'm Lucius Junius Brutus, master mage of Rome."

"Yes," Demetria said, but it didn't sound as if she was convinced of Lucius' answer. "I wonder."

"Wonder what?"

"We've seen riddles before. This may mean something more than just, 'I know my name, I know my father.'"

Now it was Lucius' turn to ponder the thought. He wiped his sandals on his cloak and put them on again, without coming to a conclusion. "There looks to be a kind of path." He pointed. "You see?"

It was true. The water came out in a wide, noisy gush, but to the side of it was a gravel margin, dry, as far as it could be seen.

Demetria raised her hands to the sky. "Apollo, great god, hear us now. We seek to know ourselves—as far as we can. Help us in this task, help us to find that which we need to save our people."

"Well prayed," said Lucius. He took out a grammarstone and said, "*O hirundon viam gemmais ostendens.*" *I summon a swallow showing the way to the jewel of Apollo.*

Lucius tossed the stone into the air, and in a flash of light a bird appeared, with shining blue tail feathers, easy to see in the grammarlight. It flew into the cavern and, fluttering and circling (for the ceiling was very tall there), waited for the youths to follow.

"By Hercules! A good choice!" Demetria said. "So small and quick!"

"If the way gets narrow, it will still be able to guide us to the jewel."

Demetria nodded and they set out.

At first it was relatively easy going. The ceiling was almost but not quite taller than the light projected, and the path was soft and level. The bird flew ahead of them, its chittering telling them where it was as it went forward and out of sight, then returning and circling the edges of the ceiling.

But soon there came a more insistent rushing sound to the water from up ahead. The stream began to go over higher and higher cascades, plashing on rocks and small boulders. They had to clamber around and over these and finally to help each other up rock faces. The ceiling also lowered, to the point where the swallow stopped hovering and mostly perched on an outcrop before going forward.

After a particularly challenging climb, Lucius and Demetria both took a moment to catch their breath and dust off their tunics. That's when they saw the second message.

"*Meden agan*," read Demetria. "Nothing too much." It was carved into a rock wall that went up to the ceiling. The stream came out of a hole in the wall, big enough to crawl into but not to walk upright in. The swallow alit next to the outlet of the water.

"Nothing too much! Another riddle," Lucius said.

"It's good advice," Demetria said. "Don't go to extremes. Of course I seldom follow it."

Lucius counted on his fingers. "One, know yourself. Two, don't go to extremes. Together, the messages seem to mean 'keep your wits about you.'"

"True. Which is good in a cavern where, so Helioxenus' mother said, there are 'guardians.' Of what, I wonder?"

"Let's go," said Lucius. "The night will soon be spent and we must account for where we've been."

The bird cried out as it flew into the hole, almost as if to say, "I'm brave!" and the youths soon followed, the light projecting up several paces ahead of them.

The passageway slanted up gently, sometimes allowing the youths to walk stooped over, other times to crawl almost with their heads brushing the ceiling. No one path kept them dry, so they ended up quite soaked and muddy by the time they came to the end of it.

The echoes of chittering ahead told them they had come to a larger cavern again.

But the bird was not all they heard. A low roar signaled a cascade, and so it was: a taller cascade than any of the others. It may have been the height of three tall men, and it came out in a shower, with a flat rock as its base.

"Wash off in that," Demetria advised, pointing.

"If only there were a way to get dry," Lucius said. He squeezed water out of the hem of his tunic.

"How many grammarstones do you have left?"

"Let's see what's at the top of this first."

They could have used a grammar to fly up, but they did find a way to climb, though at the expense of scraped knuckles and knees.

"Just remember, if we need to retreat, there's no jumping from there," Demetria said when they had finally made their way to the top.

"I don't plan to retreat," Lucius said.

"Know yourself. Nothing too much."

They directed their attention ahead of them. Several paces further on, a rock wall again barred their way. The stream emerged from it in three places. To the left of the holes, a final message: nothing more than the letter E.

"Look!" Lucius was the first to see it, and instead of pointing, walked swiftly toward it.

"In Greek, that's the letter epsilon. And it also means the number 5," said Demetria, who was trained to count and record the inventory of her father's merchandise.

Lucius stopped a few feet from it. "Or is it part of something longer that's been lost or fallen away from the wall?"

Demetria also leaned in. "It doesn't look like it." The E was almost at eye level for them, and it was easy to see in the grammarlight that the natural stone was undisturbed around the carving.

When they looked away, the letter seemed burned into their mind's eye, swimming before them in the air.

"I wonder what it can mean?" Lucius said finally.

"It doesn't mean Apollo; that begins with an alpha," Demetria said.

"And it doesn't start with the letter of any of the Olympians."

"Unless you count Hestia."

"But Helioxenus said—"

"It could be anything."

"Or nothing."

That was the end of the conversation for the moment. They both looked up at the wall, which went up for some distance, nearly a sheer face, no knobs or outcrops that could be climbed. The holes in the wall resembled each other: just large enough for the water to come out in a steady gush. If they wanted to go farther up, they would have to immerse themselves and crawl.

"Is there no other way?" Demetria said when they had well and truly examined every crack and cranny in the wall.

"I could make a grammar that cracks the wall open," Lucius suggested.

"I don't think Apollo would be so keen on that. And what about the guardians of which Helioxenus' mother spoke? If you attack Apollo's stronghold, someone no doubt will fly to its aid."

"E. I wonder," Lucius said. Then he cocked his head, rotating it to the right.

"What is it?"

Lucius knelt. "Ask the gods' help that I do not catch cold and die," he said.

"You're not going in there? You don't know how far it is. There may be no place to breathe."

"I think there is." And with that, he plunged into the stream and scrambled out of sight.

"Lucius! Why don't you ever tell me anything?" Demetria cried.

An agonizing wait—short, but seeming a very long time—ensued. Demetria could have gone in after him, but she had no idea what he was intending to do. She thanked the gods when he emerged, wet from head to toe, but with a triumphant smile on his face.

"As I thought!" he said, wiping his dripping hair out of his face. "There are three holes, are there not? And there are three bars to the epsilon. Once I went into the water, I felt above me for a hole. Sure enough, one came almost immediately. I stood up—it was big enough for both of us to stand in—and I found the connecting bar. The epsilon is the way for us to get through, Demetria. We just need to climb into the hole with the connecting bar and keep going!"

Demetria shook her head. "An epsilon on its side, with the three bars pointing down instead of to the right, and the connecting bar over them rather than to their left!"

"Exactly!"

"Perhaps you are not as great a simpleton as I thought."

"Hold on to my foot," Lucius said. "It's not far."

It was true. The youths crawled, holding their breath, for a time, then pushed their heads above water to draw in air. It was nearly impossible—the water rose almost to the top of the hole it had carved. But after they had surfaced twice, the ceiling of the rock disappeared entirely. First Lucius, then Demetria stood up in the hole that Lucius had correctly said was one of the bars of the epsilon. The connecting bar, another small hole or cavern, was accessible by a short climb using natural hand and footholds.

Once they were in this space, they continued on crawling, for it was hardly taller than the hole cut for the water. The floor of it was smooth, as if it had been carved. And just a bit further on, the light of the grammarstone began to mix with another, more colorful light.

Could it be the gem? They both wondered.

They would find out very soon.

::XXIII::

Just a few more paces' crawl, and they emerged into a vast cavern, so big the grammarlight seemed only a pinpoint in it.

And only a pinpoint it was, compared to the iridescent scales of green, gold, blue and red which sparkled from the inhabitant of the cavern.

The scales told them it was something like a serpent, but much, much bigger. It sat on its own massive coils and its head was as big as a treasury house of Delphi, the mouth as big as a door, and flanked by fangs as long as the marble columns of those treasuries.

Indeed, Lucius and Demetria both thought of a serpent at first, because the monster had no arms or legs like a lizard, but it was so big it must be considered, well, a dragon, for its head was adorned with feathers of blazing colors and it had feathered wings as well, furled now but, when open, the length of two sailing ships.

It gazed down at them thoughtfully, with eyes the pupils of which were as large as warriors' shields. It was difficult not to get lost in those eyes, for they immediately told the youths without speaking that their owner was unimaginably old and wise.

"My name is Pytho," it said after a time. It did not seem to speak Greek or Latin, but its own language that the youths were able to understand nevertheless. "Welcome. You have come this far. Outstanding. That makes you worthy, children." Its voice was deep, sibilant, resounding, and yet somehow quiet and almost reassuring. Its eyes glittered, full both of wisdom and now, they saw, a kind of laughter.

Lucius' teeth were now chattering and his knees weak, but he still managed to speak. "Pytho—we've heard your story. Apollo slew you. Are you only a spirit?" He was hoping to be right, because a real serpent as big as this one would make short work of both him and Demetria. And there would be no retreat, of course. The dragon only needed to extend its head a little ways to pluck the both of them off the ground with its huge front fangs, long before they could scramble back into the connecting bar of the epsilon.

A little rumble like a laugh emanated from Pytho's throat. "No, child. I am very real. The stories are half-true. Yes, I am the great she-dragon who once ruled over Delphi. The young god, so they say, killed me. But I am immortal."

"But we saw your bones underneath the temple!" Lucius said.

"Did you?" Another indulgent laugh emanated from Pytho's enormous jaws. "What a convenient thing, to know where one's enemy's bones are. But those are not my bones. Some other ancient unfortunate is buried there."

Demetria said, "But then..."

"It is true," continued Pytho, "that Apollo's arrows brought me so low that I would have died if I could have. I am a thousand years old, but the plague on the arrow-points made me fall unconscious. And so he imprisoned me here, bound with curses, never to return to the upper air. Unless..." and here the dragon trailed off, seemingly lost in thought.

In the silence Demetria felt encouraged to ask the proper question: "Do you have my jewel?"

Pytho's eyes lit up eagerly. "Yes, I do, child. It came to me on the stream not long ago. Hephaestus' work, and very pretty it is. It is well named, though it has not seen nearly as much as I have."

Now Demetria remembered that the priestess had called the jewel the Eye of Pytho. Was it hers, then? But Hephaestus had made it. It was not Pytho's true way of seeing. She wanted to ask Pytho about this, but dared not.

"The jewel is ours. We've come to retrieve it," Demetria said, speaking as forcefully as her fear allowed. "You must give it back and let us go our way. We have no quarrel with you nor are we servants of Apollo. We are from Rome and our quest is to save it from the slavery of the Etruscans."

"Rome! Etruscans! Very important, very important, child. I am sure your quest is of the gravest importance." The dragon lowered its head a little toward the youths, as if to whisper, though it could not if it tried. "Here, now. I am prepared to give you the jewel, certainly. But in return you must give me my freedom."

"How so?" asked Lucius, suspicious and now somewhat emboldened.

"There are three curses laid on this chamber by Apollo. If I know what they are and how to undo them, then I may come out. If not, I will be here to the end of time. You know these three curses, because they have been laid out in letters, the curse of memory, round about my prison, and you are able to read them. All worthy children are able to read, you see."

Lucius wasn't quite sure he should say anything back to the serpent, but her wise eyes compelled him. He decided, instead of telling her anything, he would ask a question. "If Apollo doesn't want you to leave, why should we tell you the three?"

"So you know them!"

"Maybe, maybe not." Demetria this time. She was trying her best not to say anything, either.

The dragon pivoted its head toward Demetria. "Certainly you know them, Greek girl. It is easy to see what a human knows and does not know. The question is, what are they? And indeed, if you are, as you say, not servants of Apollo, there is no reason why you should not give them to me."

"Not servants, but allies," Demetria said. "I am Greek. If Apollo has imprisoned you here, there must be a good reason he has cursed you."

"That is where you are wrong, child," said Pytho, and for the first time the tone of her voice began to resemble the menace of her fangs. "Apollo is a foreign god. I am more Greek than the Greeks. I am of this land originally. Apollo invaded from another place."

Demetria didn't know that was so; the dragon was clever, and so intimidating that it was hard to think calmly. So she appealed to a greater power. "Surely Zeus wills that you stay here?"

Pytho hissed impatiently. "Perhaps," she said, "I should just torture it out of you. That might be simpler than reasoning

179

with children."

As the dragon considered what it might do, the youths silently turned to each other. Was there a grammar that might work against this thing? If they became invisible, no doubt it would smell them. If Lucius summoned a rock wall, Python would break through it. No weapon he could think of would pierce the sparkling scales of the dragon and, besides, if she was telling the truth, she was immortal and no one except the god would be able to hurt her.

All this came through to Demetria just in that one glance. They had been in difficult battles before, against terrible opponents, but this one might have been the greatest.

Pytho spoke again, more gently this time. "Do not be alarmed. What I say, sometimes I say because of the wrong done me. You might do the same if you had been here for hundreds of years, as I have."

Lucius and Demetria both looked up at the ceiling. It was indeed a small place for a dragon to stay a day, much less a year or a hundred!

"But I, as you say, have no quarrel with you," Pytho continued. "And I would be allies with the human race once I am free. Especially with those humans who now, like me, toil under a master not of their own choosing. And so, let me ask you, from your own free will, to tell me the three curses, and when I am free the first thing I will do will be to help you against these Etruscans who enslave your city."

Lucius now had the chance to imagine what might happen if he returned to Rome riding a flying immortal dragon. No one could resist him. With Pytho and the power of the grammarstones, he could well and truly be master of the world, and no gem would be needed.

"Yes, consider it, young man. You are of kingly bearing," said Pytho. "You are a prince in your own land, are you not?"

"What? You don't mean—" Demetria began.

Lucius' eyes had begun to shine. He took Demetria's hand. "Think of it, Demetria. With me as king and you as queen and this one as our champion, no one could stand against us. The world would be ours."

"You are not counting the gods," Demetria said, drawing her hand away.

"The gods would allow it," Pytho said quickly. "You do not see the gods every day. They are not in the world to be seen. They are away on Olympus and do not regard us."

"I think they would if you were free," Demetria retorted.

"We could be as great as the gods, Demetria," Lucius said. "Look at this one."

"Listen, Greek. He speaks wisdom."

A fear clutched Demetria's throat, seeing the faraway look in Lucius' eye, and she blundered. "Lucius! Remember! Know yourself! Nothing too much!"

"Ah yes, the first two curses. Thank you, young one."

Demetria blinked, frowning. "How do you know those are the first two?"

"Do you think me foolish? A thousand years makes a serpent wise, little child." She imitated the voice of Demetria for a moment—high-pitched and frightened. "Remember?" Then she changed back to her own voice. "Remember what? Remember something written in letters, the curse of memory, that you just read as you were making your way up here. And you of course told me that those were the first two by admitting they were. How did I know? You told me, as easy to see as Zeus' lightning bolt when a storm is on the horizon."

The dragon was terribly persuasive, especially as it towered over them with a mouth as wide as a door.

Demetria felt herself slipping, her stomach falling away from her, sweat beading on her forehead.

Lucius didn't help matters. "See, Demetria? She knows the first two, and she will find out the other easily. Let us ally with Pytho. Let us tell her the last curse."

"No!" Demetria cried. "Pytho, you may know what the curses are, but what do they mean? How do they help you become free?"

"Also the easy thought of a moment. Know thyself. Know your size, know how great you are. There is a door in this place that is as large as I am. That is what that tells me. The second tells me that the opening is not greater than I am. It is just as big as I am, not more and not less. The third is the key that will open the door."

Demetria thought this absurd, but she said nothing for fear that the dragon was right.

Lucius, however, had no such scruple. "I would like to see the nature of this key," Lucius said. "Neither she nor I can make out what it means."

"Tell me, then, and become the greatest king in the world."

"Lucius, no!" Demetria pleaded, and clutched his forearm.

But Lucius' eyes were on Pytho's. "It is the letter E."

Demetria wanted to scream but did not. Her unbelief at what Lucius had done outweighed her fear at what he might unleash.

The dragon hesitated before speaking. "E? What do you

mean, E?"

Lucius spoke quietly, confidently. "I mean E, in the Roman alphabet. It is an E. Or an epsilon in Greek."

Pytho seemed puzzled. "Roman *alphabet*. Epsilon."

Lucius said, now almost in a joking tone, "Do you not know how to read?"

"Read! Of course not!" The word seemed an insult to her. "Letters are the curse of memory. As soon as one learns how to read, one forgets. And knowledge is the greatest thing in the world. You must possess it, use it, and enjoy it. The stories I could tell you about the young time of the world! You would never want to stand up or eat or marry, but only to hear."

"So you have no knowledge of letters."

"A letter. A lie carved on a stone or a piece of wood! Less than nothing and gone in a moment!"

She puffed up her feathers dramatically and roared so loudly that the youths were both blown off their feet. It was at that moment that Lucius chambered a grammarstone.

"What are you doing?" Demetria managed to gasp, her breath taken away by the force of the echoing noise.

Lucius did not answer. He already had an idea for a grammar and was hoping it would not end up with their being eaten alive, like Odysseus' men in the cave of the Cyclops. But Odysseus' men, he reasoned, hadn't had a *baculum* and a pouch of grammarstones.

"*O epsilon mentem draconis,*" he said—*I summon an epsilon against the mind of the dragon*—and tossed the grammarstone towards Pytho. In mid-air, the grammarstone turned into a letter made of something like smoke, which flew into Pytho's open mouth.

The dragon, who had been roaring and raging and flapping its wings, abruptly quieted. A thoughtful cast came into her huge, menacing eyes.

"Quick!" cried Demetria. "It won't last long!"

He was indeed quick with his next grammar: "*Gemma Apollinis mani Graecais ventod,*" *May the jewel of Apollo be in the hand of the Greek woman on the wind.*

It took less than the blink of an eye for the jewel to appear. It flew from under the surface of the pool, first noticeable as a kind of star, reflecting the light emanating from the scales of Pytho. It was as if they were seeing it tossed into the water, but in reverse. The ripples made by the pool came from the jewel being brought from its depths rather than hitting the pool and sinking.

Smack! it went, into the hand of Demetria.

Demetria hesitated a moment, then called out, "Hephaestus, I ask that you redouble the pangs of this prison for Pytho, that we may escape unharmed."

The jewel flashed, and briefly the cavern lit up bright as day so that Pytho became intensely golden and silver in color. The eyes of both the youths were dazzled and they could not move.

Demetria managed after a moment to rise to one knee, but she had to brace herself against the rock with her hand. The glow the jewel had made was fading, though she still saw spots before her eyes. But when she looked up, all she saw was a long, silver fang—longer than she was tall.

Demetria rubbed her eyes. She scrambled away from the fang and caught sight of Lucius, who had a hand in front of his face and was peeking out between two fingers.

"What?" he managed to gasp.

It took more than a moment before her vision came clear enough to see what had happened. The fang was not just a fang—it was attached to a mouth that was attached to a head that had struck, just like a snake, and had almost gobbled them both up.

But at the very last, that head had been stopped in mid-strike.

"She's a statue!" Lucius exclaimed.

They backed against a wall of the cavern and stared, moving toward each other and linking arms. Pytho indeed had been turned either into a statue or been coated with a layer of silver and gold that stopped her from moving.

The youths did not wait to see which one was the case.

::XXIV::

Lucius and Demetria said little on the way out. They were concentrating on moving as quickly as possible. The epsilon passage, stones in their way, tight passages, hidden pools of water, all of these were the youths' only concern.

Finally they emerged into the almost greater darkness of the thicket that overhung the stream. It was chilly in that moment just before the sun began to warm the world again, and their arms turned gooseflesh with their wet tunics plastered against them.

They embraced, and didn't let go until both of them had banished their cold and their fear.

"Well done," whispered Lucius.

"You too," she replied, and neither of them surprised the other when they fell into a long kiss.

"You gave me a fright!" Demetria finally said after they unclenched.

"I'm sorry!" Lucius said. "I wanted to make her think I was on her side. I wanted her to believe me. She is so wise, I could never deceive her—unless I deceived you first, and you believed me!"

"But you weren't lying! You said exactly what Apollo wrote."

"Yes! It was an excellent stratagem on Apollo's part."

"Stratagem, was it?"

"Of course. Apollo knew that Pytho would understand a curse that could be put into words—know thyself, nothing in excess—words that could be spoken. But a letter, by itself? It would mean nothing to her."

"And it still does," Demetria said. "Except..."

"Except that it was the way we got in."

"And so it is probably the way out for her, if only she could squeeze herself through."

"We shall never know. Still and all..." And here Lucius took her hand. "You were the one who truly saved us! But..." he paused, thinking back on the moment. "Why did you call on Hephaestus and not only Apollo? He has charge over the cavern and the prison of Pytho, I think."

Demetria's smile could almost be made out in the thinning darkness. "I didn't want Apollo to hurt Pytho. I thought of poison arrows at first. But that would have meant more pain for her, and I almost wish she could have been our friend. So—well—I tried to think of a prayer that would keep her away from us but not make her worse off."

Now it was Lucius' turn to smile. "Friend? A dragon, our friend?"

"Do you blame me for wanting to know a little of her knowledge somehow? I thought perhaps Hephaestus might fashion a metal cage around her and perhaps we could still speak with her inside it."

Lucius nodded. "I would love to hear her stories."

"But instead, he clad her in gold and silver." Demetria sighed as she thought back to the fang poised to slice her in two.

They embraced again, even longer this time, both grateful—for each other.

Lucius was the first to speak. "*Arana*. When this is over," he said, "and Rome is saved, and we are able, I want you—"

He hesitated.

Demetria had her arms around his neck. The dawn was just coming up. She could still hardly see him, but his breath was warm on her face.

"I mean, if you wish it."

"Wish what?"

"What I said before about being king and queen—I meant that. That we would be married."

"What are you saying, Lucius Junius Brutus? You are a great fool, I think!"

"I mean, by Hercules, we still have to survive and defeat the Etruscans, of course, but..."

"But this, Lucius! What about the Roman princesses you could pick from if you are the hero of Rome?"

"None of the Roman princesses I know have ever saved me from a dragon killed by Apollo!"

Demetria had to admit that was true, and gave him a kiss for it, and then they laughed, both thinking that the answer, which Demetria had not given, was "yes."

"I was just thinking," Lucius said, "that between Nauarchus and Helioxenus and the rest of the Greek men in the world, there is going to be someone for you unless I ask you first."

"You would have to ask my father. And yours would have a say, too."

"Let's go. That's for another day, and I am too tired now to think about our parents!"

They locked arms as Lucius spoke the grammar that took them into the air.

Demetria leaned into Lucius as they flew, holding him by his neck, holding his words in her heart, and holding the jewel as tight as could be in her closed fist. She'd never let it go again.

A great weariness came over her and it felt good both to be in the open air and to be next to Lucius. Still, that didn't stop her from holding the jewel tight in her hands—she'd never let it go again—and feeling its many facets.

Facets? A thought came to her just then. She opened her hand just enough to examine the jewel. As she turned it over and over, she noticed that one of the faces had gone dull. And she realized that all she had to do to know the number of prayers she could say with the jewel would equal the number of facets on it.

Silently, she counted. Eleven bright green faces like pentagons and one dull one, for a total of twelve. One mystery solved! The next question would be—which gods and goddesses are those twelve? But then, something else, something she hadn't seen—or felt—before.

As she ran her fingers over the faces, she now felt lines cut into the jewel. One face had three straight lines next to each other, with a connecting bar.

An epsilon.

Of course. Letters.

She said nothing to Lucius, because it all seemed like a dream and she almost fell asleep against his warmth. There would be time for more talk in the morning.

They arrived just as dawn came, and they separated with a tight hug and quick kiss, agreeing to meet at midday.

"And keep that jewel safe," Lucius said.

"Forever," Demetria assured him.

::XXV::

The days to the moment of the prophecy raced by. Helioxenus took charge again of his boys and continued the rehearsals of the girls, just in case something should happen to the chorus of Corinthians.

The Corinthians, for their part, looked to be quite well trained.

Titus trained for the athletic games, traveling often to Cirrha to drive the chariot for the local sponsor.

Arruns made friends with the priests of Apollo and learned much Greek, especially the poetry of the great Sappho, who had been unknown to him before.

Tragopagus, meanwhile, confessed that he had promised to buy the jewel from Helioxenus, but only because he had been told to do so in a dream by a griffin that talked.

"The griffin again!" Demetria said. "Our Etruscan friends shadow us and know our comings and goings."

"But perhaps they do not know the true power of the jewel," Lucius said. "We have not said anything about that to anyone."

"We will have to hope for the best. Regardless, the jewel is powerful and will help us."

"All you have to do is remember what you have learned from Helioxenus."

"Gods grant me that," Demetria said, and laughed.

But memory was not the only thing that would help Demetria. Days before the prophecy, she asked Lucius to meet her in secret.

"What is it?" Lucius asked.

Demetria took the jewel out of the leather pouch she'd had fashioned to hold it. Morning sun streamed in from the window of his room, making it sparkle.

"Here," Demetria said. "I've been meaning to tell you." She turned the jewel over and over. A Greek letter was clearly visible on all of the facets except one.

"They weren't there before," Demetria explained, rubbing a thumb over the blank face, "but every day they become clearer."

"There's an epsilon, Apollo's letter," Lucius said, pointing.

"Yes, but look!" She extended the jewel in her hand. "There are other letters, besides the epsilon. There are also six alphas, an eta, a pi, a zeta, and a delta."

"So, twelve faces on the jewel. Do those letters spell a word in Greek?"

"I thought of that, too, but if it does I don't know it."

"Twelve!" Lucius said again.

"Yes, twelve." She leveled her gaze at him. "The same number of Olympians, perhaps?"

"Perhaps we should start spelling."

Demetria did just that. "The zeta would be for Zeus and

the pi Poseidon."

"And the delta is either Dionysus or Demeter."

"But Demeter is the sister of Zeus and dwells on Olympus, so she must be included. Dionysus was borne of Zeus and Semele, who is not an Olympian."

"True. I would expect her rather than him."

Demetria continued to turn the jewel, pointing to the letters. "The other eta is Hera, therefore, Zeus' wife."

"Yes. And the six alphas?"

"You have Apollo, of course. Then Athena, Artemis, Aphrodite, Ares..."

"...and Hades. Though he lives under the earth, he is a brother of Zeus!"

"Yes. Finally, the epsilon, which must be Hermes, mustn't it? He is the servant of Zeus and his son and lives with him."

They congratulated themselves on their detective work, but neither of them realized that they had forgotten one crucial detail.

The day before the prophecy, Titus had his turn in the athletic competition and won both the chariot race and the wrestling.

"These Greeks are nothing compared to us Romans," he boasted. "Who should be the king of Rome, Arruns? An unroller of scrolls, or a winner in the games?"

Arruns sipped the wine that had been sent from Titus' sponsor for the celebration. "I'm sure they would crown you king here," he said drily. "Then you would not have to listen to the prophecy."

"Bah!" was the only thing Titus said in reply, and began to teach the Greeks a drinking song.

The next day dawned much as the ones before, bright and sunny, with wisps of fog in the valley. The two brothers and Lucius folded their way into spotless togas laundered by Tragopagus' wife and walked up the hill to the temple of Apollo, accompanied by many other pilgrims.

Demetria wore the dress her mother had packed for her, along with the Eye of Pytho in a leather bag at her hip. She had her hair braided and wore a silky veil provided to her by Philocasta.

Apollodorus met them outside and explained that there would be a public sacrifice and prayers before anyone would be called up to hear the answer to their question.

Titus chafed at the delay, but finally, somewhere around an hour before noon, the Roman contingent was called into the temple, where a priest was standing in long robes that went over his feet.

The priest spoke words in Greek, which Enetius wrote down. Demetria translated the lines into Latin, with Arruns looking on:

Of those who seek to rule the land where sets the sun,
the child who kiss her first that bore him is the one.

"It is a bit mysterious," said Arruns, eyeing the priest who delivered the lines. "All jumbled together like that."

"It is the word of the god," said Apollodorus. "He speaks with divine ways. The poets capture the words of the Muses in the same way."

"Poetry!" Titus burst out. "This is as simple as simple can be! Even this one—" and he motioned at Lucius—"could figure it out. The king of Rome is the one of us two, brother, who kisses our mother first when we arrive home! We have come this far for the silliest words ever to be spoken."

"Beware," the priest rejoined, with a baleful stare at Titus. "The god has spoken. Heed his word and you shall prosper. Deny it, and your fate will seek you out."

And that was the end of the audience.

"It may not be as simple as that," Arruns said as they made their way down the steps of the temple with Apollodorus in the lead. "The one who bore us..."

"Is our mother, of course, you dunce," said Titus impatiently. "And I have nothing to fear from my fate. My fate has always been to be king of Rome after my father. Arruns, if this god says the first who kisses his mother will be king, then it must be me. I am the warrior, I am the strongest. Is it not so, Arruns?"

Arruns might have agreed several weeks ago in Rome. But the sea voyage and his friendship with the priests had changed him. It was apparent when he spoke to Demetria and Lucius on the boat, but now it came out into the open.

"Who says you are the most fit for the kingship, my brother?" he now demanded. "It is true that you are the strongest, but a king is not only a battle leader. He must also be a man of great counsel, weighing the best course for the people and the state. I am wiser than you, by an arrow's shot, Titus."

"Huh!" Titus locked his brawny arms about his brawny chest. "Wisdom! Who says you are wiser than I? In book learning, perhaps, but in matters of ruling, I am clearly better than you."

Demetria said, "Maybe you should do what I have heard

they do in Sparta. There are two kings there. One to think, and one to fight, perhaps."

"I can do the thinking and fighting for the both of us," said Titus. "Besides, the precious prophecy says nothing about two kings. There is only one first kiss, only one ruler."

"He who is king may decide to divide his power as he wills," Apollodorus pointed out. "If you wish to ask whether two kings are proper for the city of Rome, you must do that another day." He thanked the Romans for their gift to Apollo and wished them the blessings of the god.

When they were again outside the sacred precinct, with the sun shining down hot and fierce now, Arruns seemed to have changed. His face, which had been bright red with indignation, lost a bit of its color, and his voice lowered, became more measured.

"Titus is right," Arruns finally said. "He should be king. He is the strongest."

"But you just said..." Demetria protested. She and Lucius had their own plans, of course. And if Lucius respected Apollo, he would be the first to kiss his own mother (who was not the same as that of Titus and Arruns), knowing that the "fates," as the priest said, would have their way. But of Arruns or Titus, Demetria much preferred the former.

Titus turned to Demetria. "Being king is not about being wise, girl. Rome is meant to defeat its enemies, the Latins. They want to take our land and move into Etruria if they can. We are on the frontier of the motherland. Ours is a city of warriors."

"Motherland," Lucius whispered to himself. "I wonder."

Meanwhile, Arruns was shaking hands with Titus.

"Regardless of who kisses first, I have no doubt you shall rule Rome, brother. It is the best choice."

"Then you will get out of the way when we are reunited with our kin at home," Titus said.

To this Arruns nodded, but said nothing.

There was a reason for his silence. When all had retired in anticipation of the trip to Cirrha the next day for the voyage home, Arruns woke Lucius and together they knocked on Demetria's door. Once she was awakened, they went outside to Tragopagus' courtyard.

It was dark and chilly, and in any other situation the youths would have been annoyed. But this was Arruns speaking.

"I need you both to help me," he said.

"In what way?" Lucius asked.

"When we return to Rome, I want you to distract Titus and allow me to kiss the queen my mother first. If the god is as powerful as these priests make him out to be, then it will not matter how strong Titus is. I will rule. Do you not wish it, my friend?"

"Why don't you just discuss it with Titus and come to an agreement?" Lucius rubbed his eyes. "He can be made to understand."

Demetria said nothing—like Lucius, she was still heavy with sleep—but she knew that was the wrong thing to say. Lucius would not have said it if he had been fully awake.

Arruns slapped his palm with a closed fist. "No, my brother is a great blockhead with wood instead of a mind. I have never been able to reason with him. The only way is for me to go first and let the god make a way, though I have no strength for beating my brother in a fight, nor an army of my own to defend me."

"He speaks sense, Lucius," Demetria now said.

"By Hercules, I agree with you," said Lucius. He had woken up now; his whispering became more urgent. "You have asked for something from me and Demetria. Fair enough. Then you must do something for us, Arruns. If I distract Titus so that you can kiss your mother first, you must swear that if ever anyone else comes into power, you will be loyal to him."

"Such as you, perhaps, with your horses and fish?"

"Anyone."

"I will swear it, because I believe the power of Apollo, and once I become king, Apollo will uphold me."

"Good. But perhaps one day there will be two kings of Rome—of a sort."

"Of a sort. I will most likely need your help, Lucius. I hope I can count on you."

"The god will make everything come to pass."

"So he will."

::XXVI::

As the delegation from Rome had done their duty in the sacred town of Apollo, they made ready to leave.

As Demetria secured the pouch with the jewel at her side, she considered whether she should use the prayer to Poseidon for a safe journey. The trip there had had its share of adventures, adventures better avoided, in her opinion.

When she asked Lucius, he was initially for it, but then said, "What if we need Poseidon's help against Lars Nepos? Poseidon is powerful. He could give us swift horses, cause an earthquake, bring a gale of wind."

"But if we never return to Rome, we will never meet Nepos in a fight," Demetria reminded him.

Lucius nodded, but by his eyes she could tell he was still undecided. "It is a good idea," he said finally. "I just hope we don't regret it later."

"I will never again regret a safe passage over the sea," Demetria said, and made the prayer.

Poseidon was good to his word. They encountered fine weather and no pirates. The sailors had to row more because the wind was not as favorable, and the summer heat now came more consistently, so that during times of calm the sun beat down and flashed on the water, and the rowing was thirsty work. Even Titus, Arruns, and Lucius were put into service at times to relieve the sailors, and before long Lucius' shoulders began to ache from the continuous pulling of his oar. Sweat made his tunic cling to his body and his neck and arms turned dark in no time from the sun's rays.

At night, wherever they made landfall, he and Demetria would discuss strategy for defeating Lars Nepos. Helioxenus had given them much knowledge about what could be asked of the gods, but Demetria felt she still had much to learn.

The one troublesome thing was the griffin of Nepos. They had lost Uchtave and his mirror, but the muscular Etruscan haruspex had found a way to keep sight of the youths through his magical creature. The winged lion-eagle accompanied them back to Rome, almost always visible off to the starboard, or circling about them in wide, lazy arcs.

The sharp-eyed helmsman, Kalanemos, was the first of the Greek crew to notice the griffin, and he swore an oath against bad luck that Nauarchus heard. Soon the whole ship was monitoring the flight of the monster, marveling at its gold and silver wings, and wondering at its purpose.

"Will it attack us?" Nauarchus asked Lucius and Demetria privately after a few hours' sailing from Cirrha.

"If it does, it will have my *baculum* to contend with," Lucius said.

"You would reveal yourself to Titus?" Demetria asked.

"I would have to."

As the ship knifed through the waters, shearing off white foam like wool, Lucius contemplated the possibilities. Would Nepos simply attempt to destroy the whole ship, with all three princes aboard? What was his ultimate aim in sending them off to Greece? Did he hope they would shipwreck and never return? Or did he know what Apollo would prophesy, and did he want Titus to be the next king?

He spoke with Demetria when he could, and at one of these times, she suggested that she use one of her prayers to destroy the griffin.

"We have ten left," she reminded him. "The prayers to Hephaestus and Poseidon are made. I could ask Zeus to bring lightning from the sky and take that monster away from us."

"I would leave the lightning till later," Lucius said. "It is good that we know all the different divinities to whom you can pray."

I don't know what will happen when we return to Rome, but it's likely Nepos will have quite a reception planned for us. He has to know about the jewel because he tried to steal it."

Demetria nodded and ran a finger over the bump that the jewel made in the pouch. "Whatever happens, we will do it together," she said.

"Together," Lucius said.

::XXVII::

Two days later, Nauarchus made an announcement. "Ostia off the starboard bow," he said, pointing. "We are within sight of the Roman fatherland."

"And motherland," Titus said with a broad smile. "Finally we will have the chance to greet her. I have waited longer for very few things in my life."

Arruns nodded. "It will be good to see our family again. No doubt Sextus has been gaining glory in the war against the Rutulians."

"You mean with the help of the gods we will not have lost the war and Rome is still standing, not burned to the ground," Titus went on. "Such is the skill of Sextus as a general."

The ship maneuvered into the mouth of the Tiber and dropped anchor as Titus and Arruns argued about what to do. It was late afternoon and twenty miles lay between the town of Ostia and Rome.

"I will take a horse and ride there," Titus said. "I can be there well before nightfall. You do not need to be with me when I greet our mother. Besides, you hate riding anyway."

Arruns surprised Titus with his reply. "I will go with you, brother. We are family, after all."

"You are as foolish as this one, here," Titus said, pointing at Lucius.

Arruns looked meaningfully at Lucius, who shrugged his shoulders.

Demetria said, "We must all go together. The king sent Lucius as the bearer of truth. He will want to hear from him. We can take a barge up the river tomorrow and save the trouble of horses. It is getting late now."

Titus grumbled at the idea of being delayed, but he agreed finally that the king would be impatient if Lucius were not there with the rest of them.

A fisherman took them to shore in a small boat and he told them, as fishermen often do, of the rain that had come the night before.

"Jupiter Pluvius visited here, but not down the coast," he said. "It was as if one puff of cloud come up just for us and down south, nothing."

Demetria laughed to herself, thinking how considerate Poseidon was to persuade Zeus to keep them dry and thus keep his promise.

As they walked from the beach to the small collection of houses that made up the town, there were standing puddles.

"Mind the mud, simpleton!" Titus advised Lucius. "You are going to walk straight into it."

Lucius appeared not to hear Titus. He walked through a slippery patch of ground and his legs went out from under him. In less time than it would have taken to warn him again, he was face down in the mud.

"What did I tell you!" Titus roared.

Demetria was at his side in a second, along with two crewmembers, but he waved them away, getting up.

And stumbled again.

Now, when he stood up and showed his face, it was brown with muck, but he was not annoyed: not at all.

Lucius Junius Brutus was smiling.

"Mud tastes good," he said.

Titus rolled his eyes. "For the entire trip he manages to keep the dirt off his face, and now this."

Demetria spoke to him as soon as they were able. "What was that all about?"

"I just kissed my mother."

"What?"

"The prophecy. If I'm right, it was not as simple as Titus likes to think. The prophecy didn't say, 'The first to kiss his mother will have the throne.' It said, 'who bore him.'"

"Well, isn't that one's mother?"

"It could be. But isn't the earth the mother of us all? That is our true mother. And that is what I kissed."

"Lucius Junius Brutus, you are a simpleton."

"Don't you think it more likely than what Titus and Arruns are now preparing to do?"

"That's not why you are a simpleton."

Lucius stood there dumbly, feeling more and more like a simpleton as Demetria stared at him.

"You've got to start telling me your plans before you do them!" she cried. "If you truly want me to marry you."

"I..." Lucius could think of nothing to say. He would've said that he kept it from her because he didn't want anyone else to know until after he had done it. But of course she would've scolded him for not believing she could keep a secret.

She twined her arms around his neck. "There is something about you I can't understand. Why you don't trust me."

"I do trust you."

"Not enough." She locked eyes with him. "I will kiss you now. It is the last chance we will have before returning to Rome."

"But there is still mud on my face."

She leaned in and kissed him, holding her face in his hands. When she drew back, there was dirt on her cheeks.

"You're muddy now, too."

"That is the point, simpleton. We are together, both in the mud and out of it."

Then he kissed her back.

They spent the night in the best house of the best man of Ostia, who was honored to take them in. The next day, they hired a barge to take them back to Rome, while a messenger rode on ahead to inform the king that they had arrived.

When they reached the shallows of the River Tiber where cargo was unloaded, almost no one from the city was there to greet them. In fact, the whole dockyard was full of barrels and boxes of cargo, but no one was hauling it away.

"What is the matter?" Arruns asked one of the few dockworkers still in the area.

"Tarquin has the whole population of Rome working. We are building the Cloaca Maxima."

"What? Has he gone insane?"

"Some say he has. Nevertheless, we all, old and young, rich and poor Romans, have been sent to dig ditches and lay stones for the drainage of the city."

"All Romans?" Demetria asked.

"All except foreigners, who are not citizens, and those of Etruscan descent. I am from Falerni, across the river and to the north. We do not work."

"This is madness," Arruns said.

"Maybe not," Titus rejoined. "Father might have some important plan."

Or perhaps Lars Nepos is the one behind it, Lucius thought. He leaned on his *baculum* as they climbed the steep slope up from the river, past a gate on the wooden palisade wall of the city, and toward the area of the Forum, past the Greek quarter where Demetria's parents lived.

On a small knoll, a spur of the Aventine Hill, the southernmost of the seven hills of Rome, they got their first chance to see the middle of the city. Hundreds of people, both men, women, and children, could be seen with spades and baskets, either digging or hauling away dirt. Fully armored soldiers stood with them, holding spears upright, or gesturing with shortswords. their helmets with their crests bright in the sun.

It was all Lucius could do not to cry out in wrath and indignation.

They threaded their way through the muddy streets. Everywhere, it seemed, ran channels to dig and drain. The hot sun beat down and the people working wore pained expressions and seemed to plead with the princes as they made their way up to the Palatine Hill. It was stiflingly hot, but humid in the low-lying area of the Forum. Many of the channels had standing water in them.

Then suddenly a breeze came from nowhere, and the temperature dropped rapidly. The sun disappeared behind clouds that had not been there a moment ago. Then, most astonishingly, it began to snow: big fluffy flakes that alit on everything and melted as soon as they touched.

"By Jupiter!" Titus whispered. Then he cried, "Stop work! Stop work!"

Those around Titus left off from their spades and baskets. In truth, they would have stopped anyway, for the snow kept on falling.

"It is a prodigy! Go to your homes and wait for the haruspex to interpret it! No more work, Romans. No more work today."

The whole company exchanged looks of astonishment, except for Lucius, of course, who put his hand out to catch a falling snowflake.

"Let us hasten to the king," Arruns said. "A stranger day I have never seen."

Titus led the way and soon was well ahead of the rest of them. Arruns tried his best to keep up, but his newfound strength was not enough. He kept motioning Lucius and Demetria to follow, still hopeful he would be able to kiss his mother before Titus.

Meanwhile, Lucius had his eye on Demetria. "Now you are the one not telling me things," he whispered to her during a quiet moment. "Did you call on Zeus?"

"Yes. I couldn't have those poor folk continue on like that. They are free Romans, not slaves."

"But that's one very powerful god we cannot call on to defeat Nepos."

"Nevertheless. Trust me, Lucius. You can do this. We—" she paused just for a moment. "—can do this."

"With the gods' help!"

Demetria looked all about her. The snow continued to fall; Romans continued to disperse to their homes. "Don't you think—" she began, but Lucius cut her off.

"Yes, I do," he said. "Thank you. For today, we've stopped a great injustice. And we need to find out why it's being done."

They proceeded up as best they could amidst the diggings to the king's residence on the Palatine.

Arruns hung back a moment to speak with Lucius. "A disturbance. I'm sure you can manage it, as you managed the snow just now."

"That wasn't me," Lucius said.

"Still and all."

The house of the king was unusually quiet. Though the reception hall was guarded, as usual, no slaves were to be seen all through the first floor.

The four travelers took the narrow staircase leading to the king's private suite of rooms, only to meet Lars Nepos, at the top of the stairs, standing outside the door in the hallway.

"Where are Father and Mother? We would greet them," Titus said.

"They are busy with great matters," said Nepos.

Titus reddened. "Greater matters than greeting their flesh and blood after a long separation? Are you mad, liver-looker?"

Nepos tapped his mirror on his open palm. He was taller than Titus and almost as muscular, and though younger, gave the appearance of great wisdom.

"Do not be so impatient, prince."

"Stand aside from the door, Nepos," Titus said. "I will go in to my mother and father. It is not for you to bar me."

Nepos didn't budge.

Arruns said, "Titus, wait a moment."

Titus shook his head and said nothing, striding forward on powerful legs. He reached out to grab Nepos by the cloak or the neck and push him aside, the way he might do with any of the servants of the king in the palace. But he never got close to doing what he wanted.

Nepos seized Titus by the forearm. He could do that because his hands and fingers were quite large. Once he had Titus in his grip, he pulled down on the arm, bringing Titus with him.

"By Mars!" Titus gasped, bent over at the small of his back.

Nepos' hat went askew, but that was all that indicated he was exerting himself in any way.

Arruns was frozen where he stood.

Lucius pulled the staff from its cornel wood sheath.

"No!" Demetria whispered. "Not here!"

But Lucius was already chambering a grammarstone.

Titus groaned in pain, still doubled over, his free arm flailing and unable to be used.

Nepos brought his mirror around to Titus' thigh and measured it against a spike on the frame, then pulled it back to strike.

"*Manus haruspicis infirmae factae,*" Lucius said, and cast a grammarstone. *May the hands of the haruspex be made weak.*

Titus broke free.

The mirror dropped on the ground.

Nepos stood up straight, holding his hands out in front of

him.

"Well done!" Arruns cried.

Titus stumbled back, panting. "What in the name of all the gods...?" he managed to say.

Nepos used his forearm to reposition his hat. He was breathing hard and face red, but the expression on his face was one of hatred rather than fear. "You win this round, Brutus," he said. "But it is a hollow victory."

The mirror flew up into his hands, which he flexed, as if they had been asleep. "You see that your power is not as great as mine. You would do well to allow the king to be king." He turned to Titus. "You will see your parents when I choose."

"Where is Sextus?" Arruns said.

"Encamped against the Rutulians," said Nepos. "He leads the Romans valiantly."

Titus said, "I would go out against the enemy. But not until I see my mo—my father and mother."

Nepos was still breathing hard, but his color was near normal, as was his tone of voice. "You will see them. Go now to your rooms and rest. You have had a long journey. Tomorrow there will be plenty of time for reunions."

Titus scowled but left the room without a word.

Arruns seemed about to speak, but after a pleading look at Demetria and Lucius he left silently as well.

"Go," Nepos said. "Go to your own house. You will find it a place of mourning. There is no need for a fight at this time."

"The king will not enslave the people of Rome," Lucius said. "Nor will you."

"Go, and you will see the reason for the hard work being done."

"Your hour is near," Lucius said as he and Demetria turned to go.

On the short walk between hills, Lucius was not in the mood for talk.

"We need to strike him as soon as possible," Demetria said. "Your grammarstone availed against him. We know your power is strong."

Lucius nodded, but said nothing.

Demetria soon found out why Lucius had been so tight-lipped. They did find the Junius household a place of mourning.

"Father!" Lucius cried when told the news.

"He contracted a fever," Mother said. They were in the atrium, surrounded by slaves. "It was malaria. It is the swampy places in the Forum that causes it."

"But he is too old to contract it!" Lucius said. "It does not take those who have been exposed to it for so long."

"This is true. But the gods take whom they will."

"Mother." Lucius embraced her, his head against her neck.

"And all the Romans working—rich and poor together?" Demetria asked.

"The way it has been told, Tarquin became so agitated about Father's death that he decided to get rid of the swamps once and for all. It is the swamp that causes the fever; we know this. So the king wants to dry out the Forum, put stone channels everywhere to take away the water, and cover over the channels as well."

Demetria shook her head. "And so Father's death is the cause of all this?"

"Yes. That is what is being said about it."

Now Lucius pulled away and spoke, hot with anger. "How do we know that the fever was not a poison, or a magic curse, sent upon Father to get him out of the way of the kingship?"

"We do not know that," Junia said. "But Father was not to be king. He is Roman. You know that. There are three sons and you in line to succeed Tarquinius."

"But he could be king if Rome takes back her own land."

"Rome cannot stand against the might of Etruria, Lucius."

"Yes, we can." Lucius balled his fists. "And we are going to."

::XXVIII::

Lucius left the house at a run.

"Do you know what you're doing?" Demetria called after him.

Lucius barely slowed as he spoke over his left shoulder. "My father died and he didn't even know I was in my right mind. I am going to destroy the person responsible for that."

"I will strike him with a disease. Apollo can do this. I can still pray to him."

"No. This is my fight."

"If you fight it by yourself, you—" Demetria hadn't the heart to finish. Lucius was in a fury at Nepos. She could see that. Being told he couldn't kill the haruspex himself would only further enrage him.

They were on their way back through the diggings of the Cloaca Maxima. In the distance, between two cornel trees on the hillside of the Palatine, a figure came into sight, holding something glowing.

"*O aper haruspicem*," Lucius said, *I summon a wild boar against the haruspex*, and cast a grammarstone.

Boars, with their enormous tusks, bad temper, and swift feet, were formidable opponents even to groups of men with spears. The one that Lucius created was all of these things.

It sprinted fast on its short legs around the holes in the ground, leaping at times when it needed to, straight for Nepos, who stood calmly on the incline of the hill.

Demetria had her doubts about Lucius' decision. She and he both knew that the magic mirrors of the Etruscans were best at defense, especially when they could see an enemy coming.

And so it was. When the boar came close enough that it would've been able to see the mirror flashing in front of it, it reversed course—not turning around, but simply shifting, in an instant, from going toward Nepos to going away from him. That was the power of the mirror: to reflect, deflect, turn away.

Now the boar came straight for Lucius and Demetria.

For a second, Demetria thought of using a prayer, but she knew she had a limited number of them left. Instead, she let Lucius act this time, and thankfully, he was able to think quickly.

"*O decem hastae terrai aprum adversae*," *I summon ten spears in the grounded pointed against the boar*, he said, and cast a grammarstone about twenty paces ahead of them.

Just as the boar made its final leap at them, the spears appeared in a staggered row, points up, embedded in the dirt as Lucius had asked. The boar leapt and impaled itself on the spears, roaring in its death agony as it did so.

Nepos called from across the way. "Brutus, you do me wrong."

"You killed my father."

"No, fever did that. But you killed my kin."

"Turanquil killed herself."

"You lie."

"Let my grammarstones speak truly for me, then."

And Lucius let fly a stone, speaking the following words: "*O igns liquefaciens orbem speculi haruspicis,*"*I summon fire melting the frame of the mirror of the haruspex.*" He reasoned that if he could not attack the reflecting part of the mirror, perhaps he could render it useless by destroying the means by which it was held.

In mid-air, the stone turned into a ring of fire shaped like the mirror frame, spinning end over end and giving off sparks. It clung to the frame of the mirror as if by a magnet, and heated it in an instant, so that Nepos cried out in pain and dropped it.

But before Lucius could follow up with another grammar, Nepos spoke a word and from out of the face of the mirror water gushed, putting out the magical fire of Lucius and raising a great cloud of steam.

"Lucius!" Demetria said sharply. "Let me."

"What do you have in mind?"

"Watch this," Demetria said. "I've been pondering this. You will see."

"I call on Ares to lead an irresistible army against the haruspex!" Demetria shouted, her hand on the jewel.

The prayer was effective. An uncountable host of armored men were called into being, and all of them had swords and spears. They quickly surrounded Nepos and the points of their weapons were poised to pierce him through.

But Nepos said another word, and the mirror, still on the ground and wet with steam, flashed brightly.

Demetria and Lucius would have been blinded if they had taken the attack head on. As it was, their vision was dazzled if not taken away, and the first several rows of warriors dropped their weapons and held their hands to their eyes. Because these were blocking the rest, the whole army fell into confusion.

Lucius cried, "It is as Helioxenus said! The prayer to Ares brings strength of numbers and strength of body, but not of strategy!"

"Athena, then," Demetria said. "They will work together." And she held up her gem and prayed: "Athena, goddess of battle leaders! Bring a hero who can take the army to victory!"

A hero did appear. He seemed to be picked from the back ranks of Ares' army, and he shouted, in Greek: "Back away! Shields up! Shield your eyes!"

The army responded as one, lifting their bronze circle shields to the edge of their helmets, and letting the blinded men slip through to the outer bands of the formation.

"Shields up, spears forward!" The hero yelled in a voice that carried throughout the ranks. "First rank, kneel! Second rank, throw!"

It was a good plan. Lars Nepos was still surrounded. With an entire circle of spears coming at him, he would not be able to fend all of them off with his mirror. And if some missed and came at the men on the other side of the circle, their raised shields would protect them. Surely Nepos would be skewered on two dozen spits.

But it was not so simple a task. As soon as the spears were loosed, Nepos swept with the mirror underneath him and a puff of wind lifted him above the level of their arc. All of the spears then flew straight into the shields of the men opposite.

Cries of pain told the youths that a few of the spears at least had gotten past the shields.

Then, before the hero could give another answer, something changed with the puff of wind created by the mirror that allowed Nepos to rise. It became a cloud of mist rapidly expanding. First it covered the haruspex, rising up. Then it obscured the fighting men rank by rank.

"Retreat out of the mist! Hold your spears!" the hero cried, and for a moment there was confusion as soldiers stumbled over one another stepping back. It was a good thing no one attempted to throw a spear into the air where Nepos had last been seen. The spear might disappear into the cloud, missing Nepos, and then reappearing between the eyes of a soldier with no warning.

"He must still be in there," Lucius said. He threw a grammarstone with his *baculum*, shouting, "*Nubes ventod dispersa!*" *May the cloud have been scattered by the wind.*

A fresh breeze that turned into a stiff wind blew away the cloud. But that cloud of mist was replaced with an army of gold and silver winged griffons and sphinxes.

The monsters flew in all directions. Perhaps there were twenty of them; it was difficult to say. They swooped and snapped and clawed at the army, and their jaws were big enough to tear out a man's throat if it got hold of him.

Now a great battle was joined. The soldiers outnumbered the monsters, but their spears were mostly no match for the tough hides and metallic wings of their opponents. Worse, the sphinxes, because they had the heads of men, were able to speak words of confusion, at the same time striking with their front claws and addressing the soldiers with riddles that could not be solved but also could not be ignored. Steadily the sphinxes and griffins pushed the men back toward the hero, who had created a shield-wall of bodyguards around himself and was thrusting with a sharp sword at the monsters as they swooped at him.

"How the dragon Pytho would be a help now!o Lucius cried in the confusion, though he was not sure that Demetria could hear him.

A sphinx came at him with hypnotizing eyes, sharp claws, and beating wings.

"*Sphinx suois verbois confusa!*" he managed to say as he defended himself from a swipe of a claw. *May the sphinx be confounded by her own words.*

Sure enough, the monster began to speak, a question about which was the proper answer to the prophecy of Apollo, but after a moment a puzzled expression came over its face, it alit on the ground, and was run through by the spear of one of Ares' warriors.

"Well done!" cried Demetria, who was running the facets over and over in her palm. There were fewer prayers now available to her and the most obvious ones involving attack were used. For a moment she regretted asking Poseidon for safe travel, for she knew that Nepos would have had trouble dealing with an earthquake. But she had no more than a moment's opportunity, for a griffin was flying at her with the intent to tear her limb from limb.

"I ask Artemis, the mistress of animals, for hunters with bows who can slay these wild monsters," she said, rubbing a finger over the face with a letter "A" on it. "And I ask Apollo, the farshooter, to bring death to the sphinxes who confuse and kill."

Twenty archers then appeared, each one ten feet tall and brandishing a golden bow and silver arrows. They all loosed at the same time, and they devastated the griffins and sphinxes. More than a dozen fell at the first volley.

A cheer went up from the army and from Lucius, who was readying his own grammar. He knew that attacking Nepos would mean casting a stone at him, and he knew that the mirror might reflect the grammar straight back at him. So he tried something different.

"*O spiritus haruspicis, amita Lartis Nepotis—*" *I summon the spirit of the haruspica, the aunt of Lars Nepos—*

Demetria had heard him. "What are you doing? Bringing the dead back from the grave?"

"Pray to Hades! He will help!"

"And Hermes! Leader of souls!"

"Yes, yes!"

So the youths spoke practically at the same time:

"*O spiritus haruspicis...*"

"I pray to Hades, owner of the dead, and Hermes, their guide!"

"*amita Lartis Nepotis...*"

"Bring the spirit of Turanquil here to us, to—to—"

"*molliens mentem filii sororis.*"

"—persuade Lars Nepos to give up Rome to Romans."

It was the best they could think of at the moment, and it was good that they followed up on the attack, for after the griffins and sphinxes were all shot down, the hunters disappeared, their job done, and the army of Ares and the hero of Athena were losing ground. The last men with spears threw them at Nepos, who parried them easily with his mirror, sending them back twice as fast at those who threw them. Despite her prayer that the army be irresistible and that the hero lead them to victory, it was clear Nepos' power rivaled that of the gods. Perhaps in Greece, where the worship of the Olympians was most widespread, the gods would have more power. But here in Italy, where the Etruscans were dominant, perhaps the gods of Greece could be resisted.

But now a form coalesced from nothing. It was clearly that of Turanquil, tall and powerful haruspica who had died at her own hand bringing down lightning upon herself.

But then someone else also came.

"Who?" Lucius whispered.

Nepos had finished parrying all the blows of the army. The hero, at Demetria's command, stood down.

All eyes were locked on two spirits standing before Lars Nepos.

He was bareheaded now, having lost his hat; sweat streamed down his face. His robes were torn in places, including at the sleeves, and all could see his muscular forearms, one of them scraped, perhaps from a spearpoint. His expression was unreadable. Certainly he also stared at the forms before him, but also he kept his mirror at the ready.

"Lars Nepos," said the form that was Turanquil.

"Lars Nepos," said the other form.

"Why are there two?" Demetria asked, half to herself.

Lucius thought back. Long ago, when he had been caught in the Mirror World, a double of himself and Demetria existed—their geniuses. But as the spirits became easier to see, it dawned on everyone that these spirits were of different women.

"Turanquil... sister of my mother," said Nepos. "I salute you, come from the dead. And Larthia Netiniei, sister of my father, I also salute you."

"I know what you did!" Demetria told Lucius. "You used the word *amita* to summon Turanquil. That is the word for aunt on the father's side. *Matertera*, the word I used, is the word for aunt on the mother's side. I summoned Turanquil, you summoned Larthia."

Lucius nodded. "Perhaps it will be for the good. Ready another prayer. I will have a grammarstone."

Demetria thought. There were only three faces of the jewel still bright, with the first letter of the god or goddess visible: an eta, a delta, and an alpha.

"Lars Nepos," Turanquil said, "it is time for you to yield. The power of the destiny of Rome is too great. We have fought for Etruria. We have fought for the survival of our people. But now we must let go."

"The survival of her people!" Lucius said. "The Etruscans are not threatened by the Romans. It is the other way around!"

"If the Romans gain Rome back, do you think you will be at peace with your former masters?" Demetria asked. "I sense it is not so."

Lucius had to agree and was struck with pity against his will.

"No, my aunt," said Turanquil. "We must never give up. We must carry on the heritage of our ancestors. The language, the gods, our customs. We must not allow Rome to destroy them."

Up to this point, the other spirit had been silent. Now it

spoke, in a voice that was strangely high and wavery, like an old woman's, though the spirit itself betrayed no appearance of Larthia being aged.

"Lars Nepos. Be at peace. You have already defeated the Romans, for the death of its hero is at hand. You know what to do, child. Be at peace."

Nepos seemed to straighten. A light came into his eye. He switched his stare from the spirits to Lucius.

Lucius tensed. He might have had a grammar ready, but was thinking too much about Etruscans and Romans, the future, and who would conquer whom.

Demetria had been thinking hard about the prayers remaining to her. Demeter—good if they were hungry and needed bread. Aphrodite—she could make Nepos fall in love with someone, but what good would that do? Hera. Marriage. Helioxenus had not volunteered much information about her, and the youths had not asked for it.

But while she was considering and Lucius was off-guard, Nepos acted.

He threw his mirror.

It was the last thing either of the youths expected.

The mirror came swiftly at Lucius, twirling end over end. As it twirled, it bent its course, too fast to be dodged, and caught Lucius on the top of the shoulder with one of its spikes, puncturing his tunic and opening a wound. It continued to twirl, only a little less quickly, in an arc and back into Nepos' hand.

Lucius fell to his knees and dropped the staff. The grammarstones in his hand scattered.

The spirit of Turanquil bowed its head. "It is done," it said, as if mourning.

The spirit of Larthia raised its head. "It is done!" it cried, as if exulting.

And then they both disappeared.

"The poison works quickly, Brutus," said Nepos. "You had better say a grammar before it's too late."

Lucius struggled to raise his head. "Demetria..." he managed to say. "Latin grammar... not strong enough."

She was in no state to offer a prayer. It was as if someone had pushed her off a cliff, and she was falling into a pit of fire.

But the jewel was still in her hands.

"What have I left?" she said to herself. She rotated the faces of the jewel.

"Someone else..." she muttered, her mind heavy with despair and confusion. There was someone she hadn't used, besides the three goddesses left.

"You are next, Greek, if you make any move," Nepos said. "Say your prayers to the god of the dead."

Not Hades! Demetria thought. I've already used him. But an elder Olympian, certainly!

Then Lucius' voice came to her, far off and yet so familiar. "She will be your last resort." And that of Helioxenus: "She does nothing but keep the hearth fire safe."

Fire?

"I pray to Hestia," Demetria whispered through cracked lips, even though she had no epsilon to touch on the jewel. "May she protect us with the purity of fire."

A flash of light.

Yes! Apollo's epsilon, again!

And suddenly a ring of fire surrounded both Demetria and

Lucius, not hot, as tall as the haruspex, with flames licking upwards.

"Quick!" Demetria picked herself up, knelt before Lucius, and retrieved a grammarstone from the ground, grabbing at it and catching it with her fingernails.

She put it on his lips, and he said a grammar that counteracted the poison.

Meanwhile, Nepos stood outside the ring, his angry face brightly lit. He brought up his mirror as if to throw it again, but thought better of it. The protection of Hestia must have given him pause.

Lucius was able to come to his hands and knees and grip the *baculum*. "Well done, love," he said. "We are protected—for the moment."

Just as he said this, Nepos made the mirror pulse with light to blind them again, but the flash stopped as it hit the fire and rebounded.

Nepos bent over and clutched at his face.

"He has blinded himself!" Demetria cried out.

Lucius chambered a grammarstone. "*O hasta ferrea cor haruspicis.*" *I summon an iron spearpoint against the heart of the soothsayer.*

He whirled the staff and the grammarstone flew. The fire parted for the stone, which elongated into a heavy, ash-wood shaft with a wickedly sharp leaf-shaped iron point at its end.

The spearpoint entered Nepos' chest just under his armpit, and traveled deep within.

Nepos screamed.

And fell to the ground.

::XXIX::

The mirror of the chief haruspex of Rome lay some three hand spans from him. He himself lay motionless with a spear transfixing him.

Then his hand twitched, and the mirror moved.

And stopped when Lucius pressed his foot against it.

"My mirror," Nepos managed, then coughed blood.

"You shall not have it," Lucius said. "You have done enough. You have destroyed enough."

"My death has made all things well. You know what you must do. You have it in your heart already. The spirit of my aunt has created it."

"What do you prophesy, haruspex?"

"What you already know."

Lucius shook his head. "You killed my father."

"It was necessary," Nepos said. Weakening, and almost unable to speak, he still managed a brief explanation. "To raise your anger. The gods knew all this."

Lucius said nothing more, but a tear raced down his cheek.

Demetria said, "I would ask my gods for mercy as you go

below the earth. But I know that where you go the goddess Vanth is already preparing a place. Farewell, Lars Nepos."

"Well said," the haruspex whispered, and breathed his last.

::XXX::

"The new king and queen of Rome," Arruns was saying. "That is what they are calling you."

Titus held his arms over his chest. "It appears the prophecy of Apollo was not meant for us."

They were in the reception hall of King Lucius Tarquinius: Lucius, Demetria, Arruns, Titus, and the king and queen.

"When you joined battle with the haruspex, I could not but watch!" Titus went on. "Arruns took his chance to find father and mother. They were being kept in a room and guarded, as if they were criminals!"

"I greeted mother with a kiss," said Arruns, "but not before I convinced the guards to let me through. They had been threatened by Lars Nepos."

"But now," Titus said, "it seems not to matter that you were the first to kiss Tullia."

"Now tell me, Lucius Junius Brutus," King Tarquin said, "you who have been in your right mind all this time. What was the prophecy that the god spoke to you?"

Lucius explained it, with all agreeing, and then he disclosed what he had done on reaching land in Ostia.

Titus let out a cry of admiration.

Arruns said, "You fox."

"He is very worthy of being the next king of Rome," Tarquin said. "He is half-Etruscan. And after the battle he has had, no one can oppose him. It is clear I must step aside now."

"And Demetria, the Greek, shall be his queen and consort," said Tullia. "The power of the gods has made it so!"

"And it is the will of the people," said Arruns. "They have heard of what you did for them in praying to Jupiter for the snow."

Demetria looked to Lucius, expecting him to say that he would not be king, and she not queen, but that Rome would forever after be ruled by all Romans, even if the people wanted Lucius to be king. Lucius had spent years with Logophilus writing a constitution, after all. It was all there, in Glyph's cave, carefully transcribed onto linen scrolls.

But Lucius did not say what she thought he would say.

"I will think on all this. I must go to the shrine of Numa where I am priest and put my affairs in order. Then I will come back and give everyone my decision."

He sounded very different from the Lucius she knew.

He turned to Demetria now. "Do not follow me. There is something I must do." And without even a farewell, he left the house and flew east, toward the shrine.

Demetria was dumbfounded—and then angry. Of course she would follow him! Logophilus would be there to talk Lucius out of doing anything rash—whatever that might be— but she, the supposed queen of Rome, couldn't be expected to sit by and wait while he, the supposed king of Rome, decided on something that would be better decided together.

Anyway, she had never felt compelled to obey anyone's orders, regardless of who said them!

But how should she follow? She had no grammarstones to fly, and it wouldn't do to walk anymore. Everyone knew her. They would make a parade all the way out of the city and the hiding place of the shrine would be revealed.

What else? She had prayers to three goddesses left: Aphrodite, Demeter, and Hera.

She would have to think quickly.

Lucius was thinking, too. He thought as he flew the miles in a cloudless sky, bright sunshine above him, the wind whipping his cloak. Below, fields and forests, and the occasional farmer or herdsman who would look up in wonder and point with mouth open.

They all knew him! All Rome knew he was Lucius Junius Brutus, master mage of Rome, vanquisher of Lars Nepos, who had enslaved the Roman people and killed Marcus Junius the Elder, Lucius' father.

This was the time to unveil the constitution he and Logophilus had been working on so diligently for all these years. Rome for the Romans. The plan was to create a body of men, the senate, who would make laws for the city. These would be the most educated, the wisest, from the oldest families, who loved Rome and counted it more dear than their lives. These men would hold their office for life. But also there would be new members. Men would be needed to do the business of the city: to manage the public works, keep finances in order, judge cases where the law had been broken, and protect the city by force of arms. These offices would be voted for by the people. They would be divided into thirty-five voting tribes, one for each kind and possibility, and each tribe would have a say as to which men would be put in office.

At the end of their terms, these men would be senators like the others.

In great need, the city could vote to create a dictator, a general who could lead them through a crisis. But this would be temporary. Logophilus and Lucius had decided on many other laws, but the prime one was this: that never again would there be a king in Rome.

But now that was all in doubt.

It was in doubt because of the Etruscans.

Because of what the spirit of Turanquil had said.

Was Rome really fated to destroy the Etruscan people and culture? Lucius was himself half Etruscan. He was for Rome, but he never thought he would be responsible for the death of his mother's people.

What else could be done?

He alit in the clearing next to Logophilus' casula, his modest hut, where he had lived for so long. Neither the Greek nor Kaneesh were there. It was curious, but Logophilus had many duties. He may have traveled to the nearby town of Portentia on some errand. As for the dog, she appeared and disappeared as she willed.

Lucius struggled with his contrary thoughts as he approached the cave where the ancient lore of Numa Pompilius was stored, as well as the constitution of Rome. Part of him wanted to see Logophilus, to talk over what he was thinking.

But part of him didn't.

"I am a man," Lucius told himself. "I am king of Rome. I do what I will."

Reaching the cave, he parted the screen of water that poured over its entrance: *aquam ventod, may the water be parted by wind.* It was the first grammar he'd ever heard, that had ever been perfected in his sight. So simple! And now he had done so much.

He could do more.

Lucius made light with a grammarstone. He preferred it to the smoky light given by oil lamps, and there were stones aplenty here. He did not need to save them for something else.

Something else! Yes, something else. Something where Rome and Etruria could be together, ruling the world together. He was half-Etruscan and half-Roman. Rome could be also.

The constitution was the first thing. It would need to be destroyed. He didn't like burning words, but it was necessary. That document was created before Lucius understood the true nature of the Roman destiny.

He made a turn into the workroom where scrolls and scraps of tree bark were kept for writing practice. The scrolls of the constitution should be ready at hand—

A completely unexpected sight met Lucius' eyes.

It was Logophilus, standing before him, holding up the ancile, the magic shield of Rome.

"Master," said Logo. "Welcome back from Greece."

Lucius' heart grew even more troubled. "What are you doing, Logo?"

"Protecting the constitution of Rome, master," he said.

"What? How did you—?"

"Egeria spoke with me. And we knew this might come to

pass, from the very beginning."

"Egeria? What would come to pass?"

"That you would make yourself a tyrant."

Lucius nodded. It all seemed very clear now. "You're right, Logo. This is what I must do, to preserve my mother's people. The spirit of Turanquil said it. Will Rome not one day wipe Etruria off the face of the earth?"

"This must be, Lucius. There can be only one master of Italy, one master of the world!"

Lucius' face flamed with rage. "I will be master! I will live forever with the power of grammar!" He hardly knew what he was saying, but at the same time, he had never felt so sure of anything.

"But you will not. We have worked too hard on this and the gods have willed that the people will rule in Rome."

"Stand aside, Logo. We must start over. A speech. I must write a good speech to tell the people I will rule. I will be a good king, Logo."

"A good tyrant, you mean?"

"Whatever word you use, it will not change what I do. Stand aside. I do not want to hurt you."

Logo did not move. "The shield protects the constitution of Rome."

"Does it? It is mine to take. I am the master mage."

"Take it, master, if you wish."

Lucius waved his staff. In this place of power, he did not need to cast a grammarstone. "*Ancile bracchiei magistri magi!*"

May the shield be on the arm of the master mage.

The shield did not move.

"What?" He tried again. Again, the shield stayed on Logo's

arm.

Logo: "You know that the shield was given in order to protect the city. You are speaking from your Etruscan side, to harm the city. The shield will not allow that."

Then Lucius did what he never would have done otherwise. But his anger, and now his frustration, had come to a boiling point.

"*Lapis ancile!*" he shouted, *may the stone attack the shield*, and cast a grammarstone at full speed from the *baculum*.

The stone hit the shield and bloomed into a ball of fire.

Lucius was thrown off his feet. For a moment, unbearable heat, and a smell of sulfur and of scorched hair. Smoke choked the cavern, and then the ground shook. The cavern made a roaring sound, as if it was splitting in two, or falling in on itself.

There was no way to rise, speak, or do anything but hold on.

Maybe this is best, Lucius thought, his mind reeling. Maybe the constitution can be buried and I can be buried and Tarquin will go on ruling Rome and all this will be—

He felt himself being pulled at. At first, it felt like teeth against his cloak. He heard a panting, a whining. But then a soft hand came against his cheek.

Who?

Lucius crawled in the direction where he had been pulled. He kept crawling until he heard the sound of water.

A little while later, he opened his eyes. The smoke was thinning. The curtain of water was splashing on stones before him.

And Demetria was dashing into the cave, breaking the curtain and sending a spray of water everywhere.

Some of it hit Lucius' face and revived him just enough so that he could rise to one knee.

Logo!

::XXXI::

Demetria did not exactly know that Logophilus was inside the cavern, but when she alit from the sky, carried on a soft, gauzy tapestry by a fleet of Aphrodite's doves, she heard a great boom, saw neither Lucius nor Logo, and came to the only possible conclusion.

She ran toward the source of the noise.

The idea for the flight had come to her quickly. She had woven more than one wedding veil with an image of a dove on it. It was Aphrodite's bird. A dove could fly. And so she could pray to Aphrodite to help her fly.

Aphrodite had done the rest.

Now, in the heavy smoke that smelled sour and burnt— exactly as a smashed grammarstone would—she needed to remember how the cavern was laid out.

It was no small feat. Besides the smoke, the rock was cracking, dust and stones were falling from the ceiling, and all seemed ready to collapse.

What have you done, Demetria daughter of Istocles? she thought to herself.

"Logo!" she called in Greek. "Logo! Where are you? Speak! I will hear you!"

Then she began to cough and could speak no more.

She dropped to her hands and knees, hoping the smoke would be less, and she could breathe more easily.

No such luck.

She crawled forward with her cloak over her nose, knowing she must turn left soon to enter the cavern's workroom. She didn't know what she could do for Logophilus when she found him. All she wanted to do was find him.

She redoubled her efforts, crawling, then rising halfway with the cloak still over her nose. She held out her hands, groping for anything that felt—

A hard, smooth metal surface.

She ran her hands over it. It was big, almost as tall as a man, with intricate lines cut into it at the top and bottom. Wider at the top and bottom, tapered in the middle. It was heavy, too.

Then a groan. Faint.

She pulled the Shield—for that was what it was—away from Logophilus' body. She ran her hands along it and found his face.

"Logo!" she whispered, and coughed again. "Can you walk? There isn't much time."

No answer.

What to do?

She felt for her jewel.

"Demeter," she whispered. "You are the Queen of the Earth."

It was nearly impossible in the dark to feel for the facet of the jewel that held the delta, the first sound of Demeter's name. But it was an easy shape to feel for—a triangle—and it came quickly to her fingers.

"Demeter!" she cried again. "Give us a way through the earth. Make a path through your realm, so that we may escape this smoke!"

A fissure in the rock opened. The ground gave way.

Demetria found herself tumbling downwards into darkness. Dirt found its way into her mouth, even though she was holding it tightly shut. Tree roots caught at her hair and tangled and tore it. Still she fell. She knew not whether Logophilus was tumbling with her.

"Hold on, Logo!" she tried to yell, but only got another mouthful of dirt and stones for her efforts.

After what seemed like a long time, she stopped tumbling and hit some kind of bottom. Her whole body ached, as if a crowd had been pelting her with stones. But light was coming from somewhere.

Demetria lay still for a moment, caught her breath, then felt for Logo. He was there, and what's more, he was breathing.

From up above, where she'd seen light, a sound filtered down.

The sound of cracking, crashing, and another boom.

Then silence.

Then a roaring from the hole in the ground through which they'd tumbled.

"Get up, Logo, get up!" Demetria cried.

It was no use. Logo did not move.

A wave of dirt and stone hit them full on and sent them tumbling end over end. If Demetria had ever played in the sea and been tossed head over heels by a breaker, she might have thought that was how it felt. For the earth did not bury them, but seemed to push them forward on its crest.

Quicker than it would take to say the words, Demetria and Logo flew out of the hole and into the clearing.

Demetria rolled and rolled, her momentum finally stopped by the wall that made a border for Logo's vegetable garden.

"Thank you, Goddess!" Demetria whispered, staring up into the blue sky.

When she could, she rose and went to Logophilus. His face was pale and drawn. He looked like a very old man.

"Please, live, my brother!" Demetria whispered in Greek.

Logo opened his eyes. "The constitution," he said, in Latin, very faintly.

At first, Demetria didn't know what he meant. "Consti-what?" she said.

"I lost it," he said, his voice as dry as a husk of wheat.

Finally she understood. She looked up from Logo and trained her eyes on the cavern. It had collapsed, fallen in on itself. The curtain of water was now a stream, running through broken rocks.

"Lucius!" Demetria cried.

::XXXII::

The moment that Demetria disappeared into the cave, Lucius knew what he must do.

He attempted to rise, attempted to say words that would dispel the smoke, so that Demetria could breathe, could rescue Logo, could save him from his rash actions.

He reached for his *baculum*.

It was not there.

What about a grammar, any grammar? *Ventus, ventom, venti, vento, ventod.* Wind. The wind against the smoke. *Fumo? Fumi?*

His mind reeled. "*Fumus ventom*," he said.

Nothing. The grammar was not perfect.

He could think of nothing more, but waited, hoping that Demetria would emerge from the cavern, helping Logophilus, her arm around his shoulder.

They did not emerge.

Help them! He cried to himself desperately.

And then it came to him that maybe they hadn't come out because they weren't coming out.

So he came to an important conclusion.

I have destroyed my friends. But perhaps I can preserve Rome.

And the grammar came to him, complete and perfect, that he thought needful.

Libroi... legium Romanorum... tutoi.

May the books of the Roman laws be safe.

And twelve scrolls flew out of the cavern just as it was collapsing on itself.

They flew out from under the protection of the Shield, and into Lucius' arms.

Safe.

Demetria had not seen Lucius at first because he was, in a way, the same color as the rock that had collapsed around him. He was lying prone on top of the scrolls, covered in stones and dust.

Presently he rose, gathering the scrolls in his arms, and limped away from the heap of boulders that had once been the home of the master mage of Rome.

"Lucius!" Demetria cried.

"The constitution!" Logo cried.

When Lucius reached them, he laid the scrolls at Logo's feet.

"*Aranai, gamendi,*" is all he said. *I'm sorry, friends.*

::EPILOGUE::

And so it was that Lucius Junius Brutus, Master Mage of Rome, gave up all his power. The *baculum* and the *ancile* remained buried, and the grammarstone quarry eventually became forest again.

As for Lucius, his friends forgave him, and the constitution of the city of Rome was established. Friendship between Etruscans and Romans was sworn, though it was not certain it would last. Magistrates were elected, and it fell to Lucius as his honor to be the first consul of the state of Rome, and Titus Tarquinius to be his co-consul, with Arruns elected the next year. Logophilus was named chief philosopher and interpreter of the laws.

But after that first year, Lucius refused all influence and lived a quiet life with his wife, Demetria, and their children and grandchildren.

For she had prayed to Hera, in the last prayer of the jewel of Apollo, that their family might be blessed.

And the God of Everything did the rest.

Ever afterwards, Lucius and Demetria would sit by their

fire in the city of Rome, with the temple of Jupiter Optimus Maximus above them, and the Cloaca Maxima below them, and they would say something like the following, whether in Latin or in Greek:

"Do you think the people who come after will ever believe that all that was said and done in our lives really did happen?"

And the other, gazing into the fire, would say, "No doubt it will seem as if it never could have happened."

"They will make up their own stories, and believe them."

"Yes, they will."

"Everyone believes their own stories."

And the one would put a hand over the other's hand, and they would smile, and look into the fire, and remember.

FINIS

::AUTHOR'S NOTE::

This concludes the story of Lucius Junius Brutus, Master Mage of Rome. In every one of the three books of the series, I begin by saying it is a story based on true events. But if you look into what was actually written about Lucius' life and the beginning of the Roman republic, you will see plenty of differences. The historian Titus Livius, known to us as Livy, has different villains and a different path from the last king of Rome to the beginning of the rule of the senate and people. But he agrees that the prophecy of Apollo was all-important to the story. I guess for me that's all that really matters.

As always, I benefit from the confidence and solidarity of my partner in True North Writers & Publishers Co-operative, Lyn Fairchild Hawks, and from my friends and colleagues Zac Flowerman and Ashlie Canipe. Two people, however, are most responsible for shepherding this project to completion: my wife Celeste whom I trust to be honest about what works and what doesn't in my writing, and Richard Abbott, fellow author, collaborator, and friend, to whom this book is gratefully dedicated.

243

If you would like to keep up with my future writing, ask a question, you can reach me at breakfastwithpandora.com, or at my Amazon and Goodreads author pages.

Finally, a game based on Lucius' Roman magic may be found here: http://romanmagic.kephrath.com/. *Valete!*

NOTES ON THE GREEK LANGUAGE
AND THE EYE OF PYTHO

I hope that readers had fun thinking along with Demetria as she figured out the workings of her jewel. I want to reveal to you some of the secrets behind its creation and use.

The jewel is a dodecahedron, a twelve-sided regular polygon, something like a twelve-sided die that is regularly used in fantasy role-playing games. And on every side of the jewel is a Greek letter corresponding to the first letter of the name of an Olympian divinity.

Two things might be a mystery to the reader. The first concerns the spellings of the names. Five of the divinities in the list start with an "H" when spelled in English. But there is no letter H in the Greek alphabet. The letter that looks like a capital H is actually an eta, and sounds like "ay" as in "day."

The "h" sound in Greek was not used in spellings until hundreds of years after our story, and even then was indicated by a "breathing" mark rather than a letter, which looked sort of like an apostrophe. So a name like "Hades," instead of beginning with an H, actually began with an alpha (A) in ancient Greek.

The other question lies in the number of divinities called upon in the book, which was thirteen. There were six elder Olympians—Demeter, Hades, Hera, Hestia, Poseidon, and

Zeus, along with seven younger Olympians—Apollo, Ares, Aphrodite, Artemis, Athena, Hephaestus, and Hermes.

Who was left off of the face of the dodecahedron, which had space only for 12 divinities, not 13? Hestia, of course, whose name begins with Apollo's famous epsilon. That is the answer to the riddle of the letter that is found on the temple. Hestia is also the most overlooked of the Olympians, as she is the quietest, living in the hearth fires of the ancient Greeks.

In fact, the epsilon on the temple of Apollo is one of the most enduring mysteries of the ancient world, and has never been solved.

Here is a list of the 24 letters of the Greek alphabet, along with the spellings of the Olympian divinities in Greek. See if you can determine which divinity is which, based on the list of gods and goddesses already mentioned. Two "mystery" divinities are also included in this list!

Letter	Letter name (w/pronunciation)	God or goddess
Α α	alpha (ah)	Ἅδης
		Ἀπόλλον
		Ἀθήνη
		Ἄρης
		Ἄρτεμις
		Ἀφροδίτη
Β β	beta (b)	
Γ γ	gamma (g)	
Δ δ	delta (d)	Δημήτηρ

		Διονύσος
Ε ε	epsilon (eh)	Ἑρμῆς
		Ἑστία
Ζ ζ	zeta (zd)	Ζεύς
Η η	eta (ay)	Ἥρα
		Ἥφαιστος
Θ θ	theta (th)	
Ι ι	iota (ee)	
Κ κ	kappa (k)	
Λ λ	lambda (l)	
Μ μ	mu (m)	
Ν ν	nu (n)	
Ξ ξ	xi (kss)	
Ο ο	omicron (oh)	
Π π	pi (p)	Περσφόνη
		Ποσειδῶν
Ρ ϱ	rho (r)	
Σ σ ς	sigma (s)	
Τ τ	tau (t)	
Υ υ	upsilon (uh)	
Φ φ	phi (f)	
Χ χ	chi (kh)	
Ψ ψ	psi (ps)	
Ω ω	omega (ohhh)	

D.W. FRAUENFELDER